"We S[...] The Baby [...] With Na[...] "That's The Cherokee Way."

Still struggling for composure, Julianne merely nodded.

"In the early days, a Cherokee baby was named in a ceremony by an elder in the community. A Beloved Woman. But things have changed. Today the father names the child."

And that was important to him, she realized. To adhere to tradition, to play a significant role in naming their baby.

"A lot of things have changed," he went on to say. "In an ancient Cherokee household, a man moved in with the woman he married, and he was restricted in his authority over the children. Now, a man is the undisputed head of the household."

She didn't know how to respond, not when his words barely applied. How could he be the head of the household when they didn't even live together?

"I want the baby to have my last name," he said.

Then marry me, Julianne thought hopelessly. Love me and marry me.

Dear Reader,

Let Silhouette Desire rejuvenate your romantic spirit in May with six new passionate, powerful and provocative love stories.

Our compelling yearlong twelve-book series DYNASTIES: THE BARONES continues with *Where There's Smoke…* (#1507) by Barbara McCauley, in which a fireman as courageous as he is gorgeous saves the life and wins the heart of a Barone heiress. Next, a domineering cowboy clashes with a mysterious woman hiding on his ranch, in *The Gentrys: Cinco* (#1508), the launch title of THE GENTRYS, a new three-book miniseries by Linda Conrad.

A night of passion brings new love to a rancher who lost his family and his leg in a tragic accident in *Cherokee Baby* (#1509) by reader favorite Sheri WhiteFeather. *Sleeping with Beauty* (#1510) by Laura Wright features a sheltered princess who slips past the defenses of a love-shy U.S. Marshal. A dynamic Texan inspires a sperm-bank-bound thirtysomething stranger to try conceiving the old-fashioned way in *The Cowboy's Baby Bargain* (#1511) by Emilie Rose, the latest title in Desire's BABY BANK theme promotion. And in *Her Convenient Millionaire* (#1512) by Gail Dayton, a pretend marriage between a Palm Beach socialite and her millionaire beau turns into real passion.

Why miss even one of these brand-new, red-hot love stories? Get all six and share in the excitement from Silhouette Desire this month.

Enjoy!

Melissa Jeglinski
Senior Editor, Silhouette Desire

Please address questions and book requests to:
Silhouette Reader Service
U.S.: 3010 Walden Ave., P.O. Box 1325, Buffalo, NY 14269
Canadian: P.O. Box 609, Fort Erie, Ont. L2A 5X3

Cherokee Baby
SHERI WHITEFEATHER

Silhouette®

Desire®

Published by Silhouette Books

America's Publisher of Contemporary Romance

SILHOUETTE BOOKS

ISBN 0-373-76509-6

CHEROKEE BABY

SHERI WHITEFEATHER

lives in Southern California and enjoys ethnic dining, American Indian powwows and visiting art galleries and vintage clothing stores near the beach. Since her one true passion is writing, she is thrilled to be a part of the Silhouette Desire line. When she isn't writing, she often reads until the wee hours of the morning.

Sheri is married to a Muscogee Creek silversmith. They have a son, a daughter and a trio of cats—domestic and wild. She loves to hear from her readers. You may write to her at: P.O. Box 17146, Anaheim, California 92817.

As writers, we often try to "become" our characters, live in their shoes, so to speak. In this case, the shoes I attempted to fill were custom-made cowboy boots belonging to Bobby Elk, a left-leg amputee. In my quest to delve into Bobby's world, I connected with some amazing people who taught me how fragile and triumphant the human spirit truly is. To Tony Barr, a foot amputee, expert horseman and e-mail friend, for explaining how Bobby would ride and train his horses. To Laurie, a lovely lady and double amputee, for sharing intimate details about her life.

To Margo Severson for phantom pain references.

To Al Pike, Teja Gilmore, Matthew Baughman and Ken Hung, the CPs who answered questions and/or took me on a tour of their prosthetics and orthotics facilities. If I made any technical errors in this book, I apologize. I studied my research notes and applied them to Bobby's life the best way I knew how.

One

Thirty-nine and counting.

Good Lord. Julianne McKenzie trailed behind her cousins, wondering why she'd agreed to let them fuss over her upcoming birthday. Not that she didn't relish the "girls only" vacation they'd agreed upon, she just didn't understand why they'd insisted on arranging one of those tongue-in-cheek, over-the-hill parties to go along with it.

What did her cousins know about turning forty? Mern and Kay were still in their early thirties, nearly a decade away from the big 4-0, from the onset of gray hair, crow's-feet and sagging rear ends.

And to top it off, they were both happily married. Julianne's philandering spouse had left her for a cliché. A younger woman. A loyal secretary, the kind middle-aged wives feared and middle-aged husbands couldn't seem to resist.

As her cousins reached the big wooden door of the lodge

at Elk Ridge Ranch, Julianne dragged her luggage up the stone path and sighed.

Her life was falling apart at the seams.

"Are you coming, Jul?" Kay called back.

She waved the brunette on. "I'll catch up."

Kay rolled her eyes. "You and Grandma's ancient suitcase. I can't believe you brought that thing."

"It's my good luck charm." And because it was nearly as old as she was, she wasn't about to trade it in for a younger model. The ugly green case, with its temperamental clasps and scuffed exterior, wasn't ready to be put out to pasture. It still had a few good years left.

And so do I, she thought as her happily married, thirty-something cousins entered the lodge without her.

In spite of her dwindling bankbook and the job she'd just lost, Julianne had come here to have fun, to enjoy the amenities this Texas guest ranch had to offer.

She climbed the wraparound porch and caught sight of a cowboy exiting the building and heading in her direction.

She tried to appear unaffected by his presence, but as he moved closer, she stole several quick, curious glances. He was, after all, the first true cowboy she'd ever seen. He even walked with the stiff, rugged gait of a horseman.

Attired in varying shades of denim, he looked dark and exotic, rough around the edges, with a straw hat dipped low on his forehead and a silver buckle glinting at his waist. Broad of shoulder and narrow of hip, he stood tall and strong.

A man's man. Or possibly a woman's dangerous fantasy.

Not hers, of course. These days, she knew better than to fantasize about the Y-chromosome gender.

"Do you need some help?" he asked, casting a courteous glance at the pea-green monstrosity in her hand.

"No, thank you."

"Are you sure? I'd be glad to carry that for you. Or send a ranch-hop out here, if you prefer. We provide all the same services as a five-star hotel."

"Honestly, I'm fine." She knew Elk Ridge Ranch wasn't designed to toughen up the city dweller. Supposedly their guests were encouraged to relax, to enjoy being pampered in a country setting. To dine on meals provided by a gourmet chef, to swim in a luxurious pool, to visit a masseuse after a day of hiking, riding or fishing. But she'd be damned if she was going to come across as a pint-size, Pennsylvania greenhorn who couldn't handle her own luggage.

Trying to appear more competent than her travel-weary appearance allowed, she flashed a small, self-assured smile.

But a second later she lost her composure, as well as her footing. Julianne McKenzie, the fantasy-free, pretending-to-be-tough divorcée, tripped and stumbled, nearly landing flat on her almost-forty behind.

With a foolish little yelp, she managed to regain her balance, but not her dignity. She dropped the suitcase and it opened upon impact, spilling a small selection of clothes.

Right at the cowboy's booted feet.

Mortified, she looked up at him and mumbled an apology. Suddenly he seemed taller, broader, bigger. And she felt small and stupid.

"Are you all right?" he asked.

Julianne nodded. The only injured party was her pride.

"Did you slip on something?"

"No. I'm just clumsy, I guess." She knelt to organize her mess.

"Let me help."

He crouched down, and Julianne froze. Her new bustier—the slinky French number Kay and Mern had insisted would boost her breasts, as well as her morale—was wedged beneath his slanted heel.

Should she say, "Excuse me"? Or just sort of yank it back before he got a good look at the lace contraption wrapped around his boot?

Too late, she thought. He was already glancing down to see what he'd stepped on, already shifting his weight, moving his foot, reaching for her bustier.

A piece of intimate apparel that came with a sheer, lightly boned bodice, under-wire cups, hook-and-eye closures and adjustable garters.

He handed it over with a polite if not proper expression, but she still wanted to curl up and die. Somehow his gentlemanly behavior only managed to intensify the mind-numbing moment.

"I'm sorry," he said.

"That's okay." Avoiding eye contact, she jammed the bustier back into her toppled suitcase, burying it beneath a pile of folded T-shirts.

Should she tell him that she'd bought it on an emotional whim? That her cousins convinced her that every woman should own one? Not to seduce a man, but to make herself feel pretty?

Oh, yeah, she thought. Go ahead and discuss your insecurities with a stranger. Explain to this hunky cowboy why you'd purchased a see-through bustier and thigh-high stockings as a birthday gift to yourself.

He reached for another dislodged garment and together they worked in silence, clearing the porch of her belongings.

Finally she closed the green case and tried to latch it, but it wouldn't budge. Some good luck charm, she thought, embarrassed by her incompetence once again.

"Would you like me to try?" He shifted from his crouched position, bending on one knee and keeping the other foot flat on the ground.

"If you wouldn't mind."

"Not at all."

He struggled with the clasps, too. But he didn't give up. Determined to come to her rescue, he continued to fiddle with the case.

When he pushed his hat back, she took the opportunity to study him. And realized he was probably as old as she was. Maybe even a tad older. His long black hair, which he wore in a single braid down his back, was threaded with a distinguished hint of silver, marking his temples. And his eyes, those exotic-shaped eyes, were branded with tiny lines, crinkling at the corners.

Gray hair and crow's-feet. And it looked damned good on him.

So did the rest of his features, she decided. The square jaw, the slightly aquiline nose, the razor-sharp cheekbones, the full, serious mouth.

"You're—" She paused as he glanced up, suddenly aware that she'd voiced her next thought out loud. "Native American."

His serious mouth tilted into a slightly amused smile. "And I'd bet my next pot of gold that you're Irish."

"Are you sure about that?" she asked, teasing him the way he teased her.

He reached out to smooth a strand of her hair away from her face. "Red hair, green eyes." He brushed her cheek, rubbing his knuckles over her skin. "A scatter of freckles. To me, that's Irish."

She met his gaze, and they stared at each other.

So intimately, she had to force herself to breathe.

Footsteps sounded somewhere nearby. The cowboy dropped his hand, but he didn't stop looking at her.

"Are you?" he asked.

She blinked. "Am I what?"

He studied her mouth. "Irish?"

"Yes." She wet her lips, wondering how it would feel to kiss him, to press her—

"What's going on here?" a masculine voice bellowed.

The cowboy flinched and Julianne nearly jumped out of her skin.

He recovered first. Adjusting his hat, he addressed the intruder. "Just helping a new guest with her fallen luggage."

The intruder laughed. "Sure looks odd. You two kneeling there on the ground."

Julianne glanced up and connected the disembodied voice with an older man. Short, paunchy and nearly bald, he wore a big, friendly smile. Another guest, she deducted.

"Yeah, I guess it does look odd." The cowboy pointed to the stubborn green case, which lay open at his side. "But I'm still working on it."

"So I see." The older man turned to Julianne. "I'm Jim Robbins. I come here every summer."

"Nice to meet you. I'm Julianne McKenzie. It's my first visit. I'll be here for a week, with my cousins."

"Then I'm sure I'll see you at the barn dance on Wednesday, if not before. I come here to fish, but the missus prods me to dance." He shifted to the cowboy. "Good luck with that, Bobby."

"Thanks, Jim."

The other guest departed, sauntering off the porch and into the dry Texas air.

Julianne looked at her companion, who concentrated on her suitcase. "So you're Bobby," she said weakly.

He nodded, then cleared his throat. "Bobby Elk. I own this place."

Bobby Elk. Elk Ridge Ranch. It was a simple enough

connection, but one that surprised her. "I thought you just worked here."

"My mistake. I should have introduced myself first. Especially to a guest." He glanced up for a second. "So, your name is Julianne McKenzie?"

"Yes."

"Glad to have you aboard, Ms. McKenzie. If there's anything you need, don't hesitate to ask."

"Thank you." Their conversation had turned professional, but she could still feel the heat between them. The mutual attraction.

While he worked on her suitcase, she studied his deft movements, his calloused fingers. And that's when she saw the gold band. The wedding ring on his left hand.

The air in her lungs whooshed out. He was married.

The son of a bitch was married, and behaving just like her ex.

How many times had she pictured her former husband flirting with his secretary? Kissing her? Holding her?

She wondered if Bobby Elk's wife knew that he checked out other women? That he gazed directly into their eyes? Touched their faces? Their hair?

God, she hated men.

"I got it," he said, closing her case with a resounding click.

And none too soon, she thought.

Julianne came to her feet. "I better go. My cousins are probably wondering what happened to me."

He stood, too, towering over her by nearly a foot. "I'll carry your bag."

She wanted to argue with him that she could do it herself, but instead she walked ahead of him, tossing a cool look over her shoulder. "Suit yourself."

She entered the lobby, a room boasting of country charm.

The walls, constructed of oak, set off a stone fireplace. A floor-to-ceiling window offered a stunning view of flowers, trees and hills.

Bobby stopped to say her name. "Ms. McKenzie?"

She turned, huffed out a breath. "Yes?"

"I offended you, didn't I?"

"Yes, Mr. Elk. You did. And I'm sure you know why."

"I'm sorry. I'm not usually so forward with the guests."

Yeah, right. "My cousins are waiting." She spotted Kay and Mern, watching her from the front desk.

"Yes, ma'am. I'll leave your bag with Maria. Our receptionist," he clarified. "She'll arrange for someone to take this to your room. Enjoy your stay."

He carried her suitcase to the counter, and Julianne studied his limp, the slight glitch in his walk. Served him right, she thought. Whatever injury he'd sustained, he deserved.

She waited until he left the lobby before she approached the reception desk.

Her cousins met her with eager faces. "So *that's* what kept you," Mern said.

"Who is he?" Kay asked, smiling like a Tasmanian devil.

Mern and Kay were sisters, one blond and one brunette, both adept at traveling. Kay already sipped a drink from the nearby bar, and Mern leaned against the long oak counter, where she'd probably been in the process of checking them into their rooms.

"That was Señor Bobby," an unfamiliar, heavily accented voice said. "He built this ranch."

Julianne turned, realizing that Maria, the Latina receptionist, had answered Kay's question.

"Handsome," Kay mused.

"Married," Julianne put in quickly. "Saw the ring myself." A simple gold band. The kind her ex used to wear.

"No, no, no." This from Maria, who waved her plump arms. Apparently she didn't mind insinuating herself into their conversation. "Señor Bobby isn't married. Not anymore." She made the sign of the cross, in a very religious, very respectful gesture. "His wife, she died. Three years ago."

The news struck Julianne like a fist. Like a hard, shameful blow.

Bobby Elk wasn't a cheat. He was a widower.

And she'd treated him like dirt.

Bobby cursed himself all the way to the barn. Nothing was going to lighten his mood, not the Texas Hill Country he'd come to cherish, the vast blue sky or the earthy scent of horses and hay misting the air.

He'd screwed up. And at his age, he knew better. First, he'd gotten aroused by Julianne McKenzie's underwear, by that sexy, little lacy thing he'd pretended not to notice. And then he'd touched her pretty, Irish skin. Which had left him aching to kiss her.

What an idiot.

Still cursing his stupidity, Bobby stalked into the breezeway barn, headed for the office and booted up his computer.

Rolling his shoulders to alleviate the stress, he confirmed his next appointment, which was still hours away.

He poured himself a cup of coffee and scanned the cluttered room. Michael had left the place a mess. Typical, he thought. His nephew had a penchant for disorganization. Unlike Bobby, who required all of his ducks in a tidy row.

He tasted the coffee, made a horrible face and spat it into the trash can at his feet.

A chuckle sounded behind him.

He turned around and glared at his nephew. At twenty-five, Michael Elk had grown into a damn fine Cherokee.

He could creep into a room without being seen or heard, but he brewed the worst damn coffee in the world.

"You're in quite a mood, Uncle."

"I offended one of our guests."

For a moment Michael just stared. "That's my job."

"That was your job when you were a smart-mouthed, bad-ass fifteen-year-old. Neither of us are supposed to offend our guests now."

The younger man poured himself a cup of the godawful coffee and sipped casually. "What'd you do?"

"I touched her. With a little too much familiarity, I suppose."

"Who is she?"

"A good-looking redhead. She just arrived today. She seemed receptive at first. But she got upset after she found out who I was. I guess she thought I was taking advantage of my position here."

Michael removed his hat and tossed it on the desk. He wore his hair long and loose, as free and wild as his half-cocked grin. "What were you doing? Trying to get laid?"

Bobby shook his head. At times Michael still acted like a smart-mouthed, bad-assed fifteen-year-old. But he knew it was a defense mechanism. Michael's troubled heart had been wounded by his missing girlfriend—a young woman who'd deliberately left town, then disappeared.

But at least the boy hadn't lost his passion, his emotion, the fire that drove him. Bobby had a few stirring moments now and then, but for the most part, he felt dead inside.

As dead as his wife.

As disconnected as his amputated leg.

"It's normal to want, Uncle. To see a woman you desire."

"I'm not looking for a lover." He missed the masculine release that came with sex, but he wasn't about to share his stumped, disfigured body with anyone. He didn't give a damn how active or athletic he was. Sex wasn't the same as riding a horse or running on a dirt path or working out in the gym.

Lovemaking required a partner. Human contact. And he couldn't give of himself. Not anymore.

"Apologize to her," Michael said.

"I did." And now the only thing left to do was to avoid Julianne McKenzie. "I'm going home for a while. I'll see you later."

"Uncle?"

"Yes?"

"You're a good man."

Bobby's chest constricted. The only love still left inside him was for Michael, for the youth he'd struggled to raise. "I'm not the champion you think I am."

"Yes, you are."

They stared at each other for a silent moment and then Bobby walked out of the barn and into the sun, unable to convince Michael that he wasn't the warrior he used to be.

As he took the path that led back to the lodge, where his truck was parked, he glanced up at the sky, looking for a picture in the clouds. A wolf or a deer. A protector of some kind.

When he saw nothing but white puffs floating in a sea of blue, he cut across the grassy terrain and spotted her in the distance.

For a second he thought she was a figment of his imagination. But the nervous jab in his stomach told him otherwise.

She was real. And headed straight toward him.

So much for avoiding Julianne McKenzie.

Her hair billowed around her shoulders like a fire-tinged halo. And suddenly he was reminded of who he was.

Robert Garrett Elk, from the *A-ni-wo-di,* the Red Paint Clan. No wonder the color of her hair fascinated him. The ancient members of his clan were noted for using red paint to attract lovers.

Her hair had put a spell on him.

"Bobby." She said his name in a soft voice.

He stopped, knowing he didn't have a choice. He couldn't just slip past her.

"Your receptionist told me I'd probably find you out here."

He glanced back at the building behind him. "I'm usually at the barn."

Julianne shifted her stance. She still wore the jeans and the simple T-shirt she'd sported earlier. But her hair, that scarlet, spellbinding hair, blew gloriously in the wind. "I owe you an apology."

"No, you don't." He jammed his hands into his pockets, thinking how small she was, just a sprite of a woman.

"But I was rude to you," she said.

"That's all right. I had it coming."

"That isn't true." She paused, took a breath. "It was a misunderstanding. I saw your ring and I assumed you were still married."

"Oh." Taken aback, he kept his hands in his pockets. He couldn't explain why he wore the wedding band Sharon had given him. He couldn't admit the truth, not to anyone but himself. "That was a logical deduction, Ms. McKenzie."

"Julianne," she corrected. "I'm so sorry about your wife."

Everything inside him went still. Dead still. He would never forget the pain and guilt that tainted Sharon's memory. "Thank you."

"I'm divorced," she offered.

"Is that good or bad?"

She shrugged. "I don't know. I haven't decided yet."

"So what brought you to Texas?" he asked, trying to ease into a simpler conversation.

"My birthday."

She made a sour face, and he found himself smiling. "That bad, huh?"

"I'll be forty."

He'd suspected as much. Although she wore her age well, he could see the maturity in her eyes, in her gestures. "You'll survive. I did. Two-and-half years ago."

"You're a man. Gray hair looks good on your gender."

And all those brilliant Irish locks looked incredible on her. "Come on. I'll walk you back to the lodge."

She gave him a suspicious look. "Are you trying to get rid of me?"

"I'm headed that way. And I assume you barely got a chance to relax. Besides, I think you left your cane in the lobby. And your granny glasses. Oh, and those dowdy housedresses old ladies wear. I'm sure I saw one in your suitcase."

"Very funny." She bumped his arm and started toward the lodge. "My cousins are going to have an over-the-hill party for me."

"Black balloons? A cake with a tombstone on it?"

"Exactly." She stopped, gazed up at him. "What did you do on your fortieth birthday?"

He tried not to flinch. He'd been emotionally ill that day, churning about the condition of his body. He remembered throwing his prosthesis across the cabin and smashing a lamp to smithereens. Although he deserved to be punished for what he'd done to Sharon, the constant reminder wasn't easy to bear. Particularly on the birthday she'd been teasing him about but hadn't lived to see.

''Quite truthfully, turning forty sucked.''

Julianne laughed. ''Now there's a man after my own heart.''

He laughed, too. Even though he could still feel the loss, the fear, the pain from that depressing birthday. ''I hated every minute of it.''

''Then I guess that makes you my forty-support buddy.''

''Yeah, I guess it does,'' he agreed. ''After all, no one should have to go through it alone.''

''Amen to that.'' She sighed, lifted her face to the sun. ''And no one should have to be subjected to a cake with a tombstone on it.''

Or bury a wife, he thought.

They continued in silence, passing several large barbecue grills, a host of shaded picnic benches and the chef's organic garden.

When they reached the lodge, Bobby pointed to the parking lot. ''I'm going that way.''

''Oh, okay. I think I'll book my first horseback-riding lesson for tomorrow. Should I do that at the reception desk?''

He nodded. ''Guess who your instructor will be?''

''You?'' she asked. ''My forty-support buddy?''

''Yep.'' He tipped his hat. ''Ancient cowboy at your service.''

''Then I'll see you tomorrow, old man.''

''You got it.''

He walked to his truck and then stopped to glance over his shoulder, to catch one more glimpse of her hair. But she was already gone, already out of sight.

He reached for his keys, wondering what Julianne McKenzie would say if he told her the truth about his wife.

That Sharon Elk had put her faith in him on the night she'd died.

On the night he'd killed her.

Two

Julianne sat on the edge of a rolling-pin bed, poring over a color brochure.

Her room at the lodge, artistically crafted from oak beams and plastered limestone, offered a cedar chest, a cypress table and multipaned windows.

The architecture, she read, was inspired by the German immigrants who'd originally settled in the Texas Hill Country, but the colorful baskets and clay pottery represented the Elk family's Cherokee roots.

Curious to know more, she scanned the back of the brochure, hoping to learn more about Bobby's family, but the rest of the information centered on the ranch.

"So, what did he say?"

Julianne glanced up. Kay sat at the table, watching her with a keen eye. Her cousins were staying in the room next door, but they seemed determined to remain by her side, probing her for details about Bobby Elk.

"He accepted my apology."

"And?" Kay prompted.

"And we talked about my birthday. About coping with turning forty. He seemed to understand how I feel."

"Did you tell him you were divorced?"

Julianne nodded. "I mentioned it."

"We think he's perfect for you." Kay shot a gleaming grin at Mern. She, too, sat at the table, but she wasn't nearly as devilish as the dark-haired Kay. Mern behaved like the innocent partner in crime, with her ladylike mannerisms and angelic gold locks. She merely inclined her head, waiting for Julianne's reaction.

Just her luck. Her cousins, who used to drive her to distraction when they were kids, had decided to play matchmakers. "And just how am I supposed to date him? I'm only going to be here for a week."

Kay spoke up again. "We were thinking more along the lines of a fling. Something fast, fulfilling and fun."

Julianne's jaw nearly dropped. "You mean, an affair? You've got to be kidding." She'd slept with one man in her entire life. And she'd been married to him. "I don't do things like that."

"Think about it, Jul. Sex with a gorgeous stranger. It's just what you need to pull you out of this slump."

Stunned by the casual suggestion, by the sheer raciness of it, she shifted her gaze between her cousins. "That's what this vacation was supposed to do."

Kay flashed her impish smile. "So, consider Bobby Elk an added bonus."

Dear God. "What about sexually transmitted diseases?"

"You can make sure there's protection available," Mern said in her quiet, no-nonsense manner. "You can keep condoms in a drawer. Or in your purse. It's possible to have a responsible affair."

"And they sell prophylactics in the gift shop," Kay added. "This place has everything. You don't even need to go into town."

Julianne's mind reeled. Her cousins had been here all of three hours and already they'd scoped out a box of condoms and a tantalizing man to go with them.

Kay reached for her diet soda, the caffeine jolt she thrived on. "It's time you got back into life, Jul. You've been divorced for two years."

She fidgeted with the brochure in her hand, trying to get her thoughts in order. The idea of making love to Bobby Elk scared the stuffing out of her.

But deep down, it thrilled her, too.

"What if I made a play for him and he turned me down?" She'd be mortified. Crushed. Destroyed.

Kay took another swig of her soda. "Come on, Jul. He's a red-blooded American male. And he's attracted to you."

"This whole thing is crazy." Julianne popped up and paced the room. Now she wanted to throttle her cousins for putting the idea in her head.

"Just think about it," Mern said.

Julianne stopped to study the blonde, noting how striking she was with her tiny waist, rounded hips and ample bust. Mern could seduce a man without even trying. And so could Kay. The brunette had a straightforward, free-spirited charm that drew men to her like magnets. No wonder they'd kept their husbands.

She plopped back onto the bed, picked up the brochure again. And when she caught sight of Bobby's name, her heart raced.

Kay finished her drink. "Let it simmer for a day or so. You don't have to rush into anything this minute."

Let it simmer? What did that mean? That she was supposed to face Bobby Elk tomorrow with sex on her mind?

"Easy for you to say." Already she was panicked about what tomorrow would bring. Panicked about just seeing Bobby, let alone imagining herself in bed with him.

The following morning Bobby woke with a start, shaking a leg no longer there.

Phantom pain, he thought. The nerves didn't know his leg was gone.

But Bobby knew. A man didn't lose a limb and suddenly forget that part of him was missing.

The phantoms rarely came anymore, so he closed his eyes, waiting out the discomfort, knowing it would eventually subside. He didn't believe in pharmaceutical pain-killers. He followed a natural path and when necessary found relief with Juniper Berry, an herb also known as Ghost Berry.

Ghost medicine for phantom pain. Sometimes the irony actually humored him. But not today. This frustrating morning, Bobby was in a ravaged mood.

He opened his eyes and cursed. Relaxing didn't seem to be an option, even though he knew it would help ease the pain.

He looked around his bedroom and took a deep breath. He lived in a log cabin that used to be a guest accommodation on the ranch. He'd given up the home he'd shared with his wife. Instead he stayed in a tiny place nestled on the side of a hill, surrounded by gnarled trees, flowers that sprouted on their own and long nights of seclusion.

When the phantoms subsided, Bobby rose and reached for his crutches. Carrying himself into the bathroom, he stared at the adaptations that had been made. Grab rails, a shower chair. They had been part of his routine for the past three years, but today they made him feel like a cripple.

Damn, but he hated self-pity.

He'd promised himself long ago that he wouldn't dwell on the "Why me?" syndrome. And he'd been doing fairly well. Until yesterday, until a pretty redhead named Julianne McKenzie arrived, stirring an attraction that toyed with his libido.

And made him wish, much too desperately, that his body was whole.

After his shower, he attached his prosthesis. It took all of five minutes, but he did it begrudgingly, hating himself, once again, for falling into the self-pity trap. He was a healthy man, active and strong, financially secure. He had a lot to be thankful for.

He spoke to the Creator every day, and the One Who Lives Above always listened. But this morning, Bobby couldn't find the emotional strength to give thanks.

On this bright summer morning, he felt like what he was—a forty-two-year-old widower—a man who'd lost his wife.

And, he added, grabbing a pair of Wrangler jeans from the dresser, a self-loathing, sex-starved amputee.

He made it to the barn by 6:00 a.m. and started a pot of coffee before Michael could do the damage. Checking his computer, he scanned his appointments, the riding lessons and guided tours the front desk had scheduled for him.

Julianne was his first lesson for the day.

Anxious, he glanced at his watch and listened to the coffee brew. He could handle this, he told himself. She would only be around for a week. And he knew how to interact with his guests, how to be a proper host.

All he had to do was relax and stop thinking about the sexual fury in his gut.

Ready for a boost of caffeine, he poured a cup of the European blend and settled into his desk.

The coffee tasted like heaven, and so did the continental

breakfast Chef Gerard had sent to his office. The old chef, who'd trained at Le Cordon Bleu in Paris, spoiled Bobby and his ranch hands every morning with oven-baked treats.

He polished off a buttered scone and checked his watch again.

Showtime, he thought, rising to play his part, to face Julianne as he would any other paying guest. A week-long stay at his ranch didn't come cheap, and he owed her the courtesy of a genuine smile.

Or as genuine as he could muster.

She was already there, seated at the bench outside the barn, her spellbinding hair secured in a girlish ponytail and tied with a silky blue ribbon.

She stood and sent him a look as sweet and warm as a candy-wrapped sun.

He approached her, thinking she looked like a fairy. She had a beguiling little dimple, eyes as green as moss and freckles sprinkled across her nose like glitter.

Forty looked cute on her, he decided. Bright and fresh.

"Morning," he said.

"Hi."

She adjusted the hem of an oversize denim jacket. The white blouse beneath it sported a touch of lace at the collar and a row of tiny blue buttons. Her jeans were a pair of comfortably worn Levi's. Her moderately priced boots looked brand-spanking-new.

"So, have you ever been on a horse?" he asked, gearing up for her lesson.

She shook her head. "I'm from Pennsylvania."

He couldn't help but grin. "They don't have horses in Pennsylvania?"

She waved her hands in a flighty gesture. "Oh, of course they do. That was dumb."

No, he thought. It was sweet. "I'm just teasing you, Julianne."

"I know." She sent him a lopsided smile. "And you're good at it, too."

He kept grinning. "You're an easy mark."

"So I can expect you to torture me with that sense of humor of yours?"

"Yes, ma'am." Having a sense of humor kept him alive, he supposed. That and his passion for horses. And of course, his paternal love for Michael.

He considered Julianne and wondered if she had any kids. Knowing it wasn't his place to question her, he didn't ask.

"Come on," he said, guiding her into the barn. "I'll introduce you to your mount."

He chose a well-mannered, highly trained gelding. They stopped in front of a box stall and he motioned to the quarter horse. "This is Sir Caballero. 'Sir Knight' in English. Most of the time we just call him Caballero."

"So, he's a boy."

"Yep." Amused, Bobby watched her warm up to the gelding. "A ten-year-old boy."

She tilted her head. "How can you tell?"

"That he's male?"

She glanced at the horse, then blushed furiously. "I was talking about his age. How can you tell how old he is?"

Still amused, he flashed a telltale grin. "I knew what you meant."

"Oh, goodness." She laughed, rolled her pretty green eyes. "You were teasing me again. I'm such a dork."

"No, you're not." She was playful, he thought. A little naive. And that girlish naiveté made him want to kiss her. To brush her lips with his, to taste the dimple in her cheek. "You're sweet."

She blinked and smiled, and the dimple imbedded even deeper. "Thank you."

Bobby moved closer and they gazed at each other. All he had to do was to lean forward and initiate the first kiss, the first sip of satisfaction.

When she moistened her lips, a shiver shot straight to his groin.

Lust, he thought. Sugarcoated lust.

Kissing Julianne wouldn't change who he was or what he'd done to Sharon. It wouldn't restore his honor or the broken vow he'd made to his wife's family.

It would only be a balm, temporary relief for what would never quit ailing him.

But that didn't make his desire, the hunger, any less real.

"Where were we?" he asked, doing his damnedest to break the spell, to get back on track, to quit staring at her mouth.

"We were..." About to kiss, Julianne thought. Or so it had seemed. But she couldn't be sure. She'd been out of practice for far too long.

"We were talking about Caballero," she said, suddenly recalling where they'd left off. "About him being a boy. And about how old he is." She turned to the horse and tried to gain control of her senses. She'd lain awake most of the night, considering an affair with Bobby.

A fun, fast, fulfilling fling.

"Oh, yeah." He turned to the horse, too. "First of all, he's a gelding, a castrated male."

Julianne merely nodded. She wasn't about to comment on the poor beast's castration.

"Caballero is a registered quarter horse," Bobby went on to say. "And his date of birth is on his papers. But a horse's teeth can determine its age. The wearing surface changes as they grow older."

"That makes sense." She reached out to stroke the gelding's nose, and the horse bobbed his approval.

Bobby glanced her way and once again their gazes locked. Softly, gently. Like a breath of spring.

Her cousins were right. She did need to get on with her life. To bask in the warmth and glory of a rough, rugged cowboy.

"Are you ready?" he asked.

To touch him? To lie beside his long-limbed, leanly muscled body?

"Yes," she said.

He reached for a nylon article hanging beside the stall. "This is a halter." He opened the door, entered the stall and buckled the horse into the headgear.

He led Caballero toward the barn door, and then stopped to say something in Spanish to a young Latino ranch hand, who looked at Julianne and nodded his head.

Once they were outside, Bobby tied the gelding to a hitching post. Julianne remained by his side, watching everything he did.

Yes, she thought. Yes. She wanted Bobby Elk. She wanted those big, calloused hands all over her.

The ranch hand appeared with a saddle and left it on a rack. Bobby thanked the young man in English and received a Spanish response.

After the ranch hand departed, he saddled the horse, explaining the process, naming the tack. Julianne listened, but now and then her mind drifted. Back to Bobby's hands. Back to the fantasy of his touch.

"What are you hoping to gain from your first lesson?" he asked, tightening the girth. "What do you want out of this?"

You, she wanted to say. "Just the basics. So I can take one of the guided tours into the hills and feel comfortable."

She paused, brushed a stray hair away from her face. A few strands were coming loose from her ponytail. "Do you give those tours?"

He nodded. "I'm taking a group out tomorrow morning."

She didn't want to share him with a group. "Can I book a private tour instead?"

"Yes, but it'll have to be on Thursday. That's the only day I'm free. My schedule is pretty tight this week."

She imagined being alone with him in the hills, surrounded by the scent of wildflowers and the warmth of the wind. "Then Thursday, it is. Now all I have to do is learn to ride."

He finished tacking up the gelding. "Are you nervous?"

She shook her head, glanced at the gold band on Bobby's finger.

"It's important to relax," he said. "To let the horse know you're in control."

As Bobby led Caballero, Julianne walked beside him, wondering how long he'd been married. Death had to be more stressful than divorce. She'd given up her wedding ring easily. Heck, she'd even considered flushing the meaningless thing down the toilet, but had opted to pawn it instead.

Once they were in the arena, she tried to clear her mind. But as she waited for the riding instruction to begin, she took an anxious breath.

Bobby studied her from her under the brim of his hat, the sun shining in his face. "I thought you weren't nervous, Julianne."

Okay, so maybe she was. But not about mounting the gelding. "Honestly, I'm fine." Just suddenly scared to death about the decision she'd made, the choice to have sex with a stranger.

This stranger, she thought, glancing at his ring once again.

"Are you sure?"

"Yes." So he missed his wife, she thought. That didn't mean he didn't play around. The man was a widower, not a saint.

He gave her a boost when she wasn't able to climb into the saddle on her own. Next, he adjusted her stirrups.

The lesson went easily from there. Bobby corrected her when she did something wrong and praised her when she did something right.

He remained in the center of the arena, the sun glinting off his belt buckle. She'd never undressed a cowboy, but she was more than willing to try.

He watched her walk the horse along the fence rail. "You've got a good seat, Julianne."

She sent him a quick smile, assuming that meant she sat a horse well.

The instruction lasted for almost two hours and when she dismounted, her legs wobbled.

Bobby caught her shoulders and suddenly they were standing only inches apart. His chest rose and fell, and when he dipped his head to look at her, their eyes met.

Julianne's mouth went dry. God, he was beautiful. A Cherokee masterpiece, with his copper skin and strong, sculpted features.

"You'll get over that," he said.

Over what? The wooziness in her knees? Or the silky sensation between her thighs? The heat of wanting him? "Are you sure?"

"Yes." He stepped back, his voice rough. Masculine. Much too husky.

Julianne attempted to steady her pulse, to give her lungs a dose of calm, even breathing. But the effort proved in vain. She wasn't going to get over Bobby Elk until she was wrapped in his arms.

Warm and wet and naked, she thought.

Free and sinful.

Engaged in the affair of a lifetime.

Three

___

Julianne had worked in clothing boutiques since her teens, progressing from salesgirl to manager. She wasn't exactly a fashion plate, but she had a keen sense of style, a knack for knowing what looked good on her.

But on this nerve-laced evening, everything she tried on fell flat.

"You look great." This came from Kay, who sat on the edge of Julianne's bed.

"I shouldn't have bought this. I'm too old for a backless dress," she responded, criticizing her appearance in a beveled mirror. She reached for the matching jacket and slipped it on, hoping it would help. "I shouldn't go braless anymore."

"Why not? You've still got perky breasts."

Of course, she did. Her breasts were too small to be anything but perky. She didn't actually have cleavage, which is why Kay and Mern had talked her into buying that padded bustier.

Maybe she should wear that tonight. Not with this dress, but with—

"Too bad your nipples aren't hard."

Julianne turned around to glare at Kay. "Knock it off. I'm nervous as it is." She hadn't worried about whether a specific guy would ask her to dance since her high school days. "What if Bobby isn't even there?"

"He owns this place, Jul. He'll be there."

"I hope so." She put on her cowboy boots, deciding they were the appropriate footwear for a barn dance.

"You could use a breath spray."

As Julianne covered her mouth, Kay reached into her purse. "For your nipples," her cousin clarified, handing over a small pump. "It'll make them hard. I read about it in a magazine."

Julianne studied the mint-flavored spray, and when she glanced up at Kay, they both burst out laughing.

Oh, what the hell? she thought, unbuttoning the front of her dress. She was out to seduce a man. And what man wouldn't notice erect nipples?

Mern arrived at Julianne's door a short time later and the three drove their rental car to the entertainment barn, a building designed for dances, casual meals and parties.

Guests were already gathered at rustic tables, sipping margaritas and chatting companionably. The chef had prepared an array of Southwestern appetizers. Julianne could see colorful trays garnished with tomatoes, peppers and cilantro leaves.

The dance floor accommodated Western-clad couples swaying to a beat provided by a country band. The room itself twinkled with white lights, giving the rugged atmosphere a touch of romance.

Julianne sat with her cousins and scanned the area for Bobby, and then made eye contact with a young man who smiled and came her way.

He resembled Bobby, with his long, lean body and jet-black hair. A relative, she decided. A member of the Elk family.

He stopped at their table. His skin wasn't quite as dark as Bobby's, but he had the same strong-boned features and rough-and-tumble appeal.

"Evening, ladies." He introduced himself as Michael Elk, then turned to Julianne. "You must be the good-looking redhead my uncle mentioned."

Stunned and flattered, she extended her hand. "Julianne McKenzie."

After they shook hands, he sat in the empty chair next to her. She reached for a corn chip and dipped it into a bowl of guacamole. "So Bobby's your uncle?"

"Yes, ma'am. And a damn good one. He gave up his rodeo career to raise me." Michael poured a margarita from the pitcher on their table and handed it to her. "He stepped in when my mother died. I was thirteen years old, and full of pi—" He paused to rethink his statement. "Pickles and vinegar. I was quite a handful."

And probably still was, she thought, catching the dark, dangerous gleam in his eye.

They talked for a few more minutes before Michael rose to mingle. "Enjoy the dance." He smiled at Kay and Mern. "Try the *sopes*," he said, pointing to a platter of small, ridged, pork-filled tortillas. "They're my favorite."

Taking his advice, Kay reached for one of the Mexican appetizers. "Hunky," she commented when he was out of earshot.

"Just like his uncle," Mern put in, nudging Julianne to glance toward the door, where Bobby had just arrived.

Instantly she became aware of her nerves, of the girlish flutter in her stomach. Taking a deep breath, she removed her jacket and placed it on the back of her chair. Suddenly she was warm. Much too warm.

Bobby looked like a mirage, a masculine shadow of denim and leather. A buckskin shirt fitted across his chest and a pair of cowboy-cut jeans hugged his hips. A Stetson, decorated with a silver hatband, shielded his eyes, creating an air of mystery.

"Did you hear that?" Kay asked.

Julianne couldn't hear anything above the pounding of her own heart.

"It's lady's choice, Jul. Go ask Bobby to dance before someone else snags him."

Lady's choice. That gave her a perfect excuse to approach him, yet as she made her way through the other guests, she wanted to turn tail and run.

She'd barely taken a moment to breathe, to calm her schoolgirl anxiety.

He glanced up and saw her, and she realized it was too late to skitter off like a jackrabbit.

"Hi, Bobby." She stopped in front of him, conjured a smile and tried to look more confident than she felt.

"Hello." His gaze traveled over her body, settled on her breasts for a millisecond and shot back up to her face.

Julianne shifted her feet. He'd noticed her protruding nipples. The twin peaks she'd blasted with Binaca.

"Do you want to dance?" she asked before she lost her nerve.

When he stalled, she knew she'd made a mistake. Apparently he didn't like forward women. Apparently the backless, braless dress had been the wrong thing to wear. Apparently—

"All right," he said.

All right. He didn't sound particularly enthused about holding her in his arms, but he'd agreed. To be polite, most likely.

Mortified, Julianne decided this potential affair was a pipe dream. A foolish notion going nowhere.

He led her onto the dance floor.

And suddenly everything changed.

Their eyes met and their bodies brushed, the music tempting them with a warm, slow, country ballad.

He slid his arms around her waist; she put her head on his shoulder. And the rest of the world seemed to disappear.

The twinkling lights flashed like a hundred wish-inspired stars glittering from an oak ceiling.

Julianne inhaled the scent from his cologne, the subtle mix of musk and man. He ran his fingers up and down her spine, caressing her bare back.

They could have been making love, she thought. Making love to music. She felt the flex of muscle, the hard, solid wall of his body swaying to accommodate hers.

He toyed with the ends of her hair. *"Gi-ga-ge-i,"* he whispered in a guttural tongue. "So red. So powerful."

She wanted to respond but she couldn't. Her entire body was melting. All over him.

When the song ended, they stood in the center of the dance floor, just holding each other. Until Bobby dropped his hands and stepped back.

"Wa-do," he said. "Thank you for the dance."

"You're welcome." Still a little dazed, she smiled. "Is that the Cherokee language?"

He nodded. "I don't speak it fluently. But my grandparents did."

"It's beautiful."

"Wa-do," he said again. "Thank you."

The band started another song, but Bobby didn't reach

for her. And she didn't reach for him. They separated, walked in opposite directions, and then turned back at the same moment to look at each other from across the room.

Giving her a connection she hadn't expected to feel. A fleeting embrace from heart to lonely heart.

On Thursday afternoon Bobby saddled his horse. He wasn't going to let last night's dance affect him. He wasn't going to obsess about the luxury of holding Julianne McKenzie, of swaying to a slow, silky song, of being immersed in the airy fragrance of her perfume.

He stole a glance at Julianne. She waited beside Caballero, with her hair blowing gently in the breeze.

Oh, hell. Who was he trying to kid? He was already obsessing about her. About the slim, sleek texture of her naked back and the erotic impression her nipples had made against her dress.

He'd gone to bed aroused and had awakened the same damned way.

He finished saddling his horse and went to Julianne. "Do you need a leg up?" he asked.

She gave Caballero a serious study. The sorrel gelding, at 15.2 hands, possessed a generous chest, a wide girth and a strongly muscled back. He made Julianne, with her petite frame and translucent skin, look like a pixie.

"I think I can make it on my own," she said.

Good girl, Bobby thought. He knew she was more than capable of climbing into the saddle.

She put her left foot in the stirrup and heaved herself up, grabbing the horn for support. The leather creaked beneath her rear.

Bobby mounted his horse on the "wrong" side, on the right rather than the left. Julianne gave him a confused look.

"I'm favoring an old injury," he said, telling her what he told anyone who was astute enough to notice. "And since it's easier for me to mount on the right, I train my horses to accommodate me." Which also included hand signals and the dispersal of his weight rather than the pressure of his legs.

Julianne merely nodded, apparently too polite to prod him for details.

Sometimes people questioned him further, and sometimes they didn't. When they did, he chalked up his "old injury" to an "accident" and nothing more.

On occasion, the truth leaked out. His staff, along with plenty of folks in town, knew that he was a below-the-knee amputee.

But so far, no one had told Julianne. Of that much, he was certain.

He glanced back at her. "Are you ready to hit the hills?"

She sat up a little straighter. "Yes, sir."

For nearly two hours they traveled a path Bobby reserved for inexperienced riders. The trails were wide and scenic, the trees tall and shady, the terrain smooth yet lush with foliage.

When they reached a grassy plain near the river, he stopped. Julianne had booked a half-day tour, which included a picnic. Most folks preferred to do this tour with a group, but Bobby knew why Julianne had chosen a private session.

She wanted to be alone with him, to relax, to talk. And he didn't mind obliging her. He enjoyed her company. And in spite of that romantic dance, he was professional enough to keep his hormones in check. At least in front of her. His private fantasies, his late-night and early-morning arousals, were his own business.

Besides, she was leaving in three days, right after her party.

Speaking of which. "I ran into your cousins this morning," he said as he dismounted. "And they talked to me about your birthday."

Julianne slid from her horse. "Oh, goodness. What did they say?"

"They asked for my advice. And I told them I wasn't too keen on the over-the-hill theme. I suggested that a classy dinner at the lodge and a night on the town might be more appropriate."

She gave him a pleased smile. "You did?"

He nodded. "There's a local honky-tonk I think you'd enjoy. It's perfect for a fortieth birthday."

"You mean I can get drunk there and forget how old I am?"

He laughed. "Yes, ma'am, you can."

"Will you come to my party, Bobby?"

He adjusted his hat to look at her, to count the freckles sprinkled across her nose, to admire the fire in her hair. "Your cousins already invited me."

"Does that mean you'll be there?"

He moved his gaze lower, taking in the column of her neck, the curve of her waist, the flare of her hip. "Yes. That's means I'll be there."

"Thank you."

"Sure." Before things got awkward, he tended the horses and gave her the task of spreading the blanket and unpacking the food.

When he joined her, she was in the process of filling their plates.

"Your chef is amazing." She handed him his lunch, a grilled chicken and pita sandwich, accompanied by several gourmet salads. "Do you eat like this all the time?"

"Except when I cook for myself." He tasted the wild rice medley, then went onto the mango and jicama concoction. "I can throw a meal together, but nothing this fancy."

"Me, neither." She eyed the dessert, a colorful array of freshly baked tarts. "I'd get fat if I lived here."

"I've learned to curb my appetite for sweets." And those sweets included women, he thought as he swallowed the food in his mouth.

She looked around, and he followed her gaze to the lull of the river and the flowers sprayed across the bank.

"It's so beautiful here," she said.

"Yes, it is." And so was she. An Irish fairy with invisible wings.

She turned her attention back to him. "I met your nephew. He speaks very fondly of you."

"Michael wasn't easy to raise, but I love him like a son. I wouldn't trade that experience for the world."

Julianne sighed. "I don't have any children. I wanted them, desperately. But it didn't happen." She picked at a piece of chicken in her sandwich. "We tried for years to have kids. And then we decided to have some tests done. Joe, my ex-husband, tested just fine. So that told us the problem was with me." She paused, sighed again. "But since our insurance didn't cover infertility, we didn't pursue it any further. I was willing to adopt, but Joe wasn't comfortable with the idea."

Bobby studied her expression, the sadness in her eyes. "I'm sorry."

"It's okay. It doesn't matter anymore. He cheated on me anyway."

"He sounds like a jerk."

"You think so?" Looking up from her sandwich, she smiled.

''Yeah, I do.'' He reached for his fork, instead of reaching for her, instead of touching her cheek.

Her smile fell. ''Our relationship had become rather mundane, I suppose. But he should have come to me. He should have told me he was unhappy.''

''How long were you married?'' Bobby asked.

''Twenty years.''

''Damn. That's a long time.''

She blew a frustrated breath. ''Too long, considering what he did. Joe was thirty-nine, pushing forty when he hopped into the sack with his twenty-year-old secretary.''

Bobby froze. His wife had been twenty when he'd met her, twenty-one when they'd married, twenty-two when she'd died.

Julianne picked at her sandwich again, tearing it into small bites. ''I know those kinds of age differences don't bother some people. But it was quite a blow to my ego. Why is it that men get away with everything?'' She ate a slice of the grilled chicken, casting the pita aside. ''Can you imagine me sleeping with a twenty-year-old? It's absurd.''

Bobby frowned, recalling his attraction to Sharon. Their age difference had made their relationship more exciting in the beginning. And more painful at the end. ''It is a double standard, I suppose.''

''No kidding.'' Julianne reached for her drink, took a small sip.

When they both fell silent, the lull of the river intensified. The wind blew a warm breeze, and the sun shone, dappling the water with specks of gold.

''I'm sorry.'' She glanced down at her plate, at her torn sandwich. ''I shouldn't have vented my frustrations out on you.''

"It's okay." At least now he understood why turning forty was such an issue with her.

"It's not okay. I feel like an idiot. Forcing you to listen to all that."

"Hey." Giving in to the need to touch, he leaned forward and lifted her chin, encouraging her to look at him. "I don't mind being your friend, Julianne."

She blinked, smiled. "You're a good man, Bobby."

He pulled his hand back. "Michael says that to me, too." But it felt different coming from her. It felt like even more of a lie.

They finished their lunch and cleaned up, working quietly. Bobby squinted at the sky, at a hawk soaring above the trees.

Julianne walked over to Caballero. "Is it a two-hour ride down the hill?"

"We're going down the same way we came up," he said by way of an explanation.

She made a face. "My butt's going to be really sore later, isn't it?"

He checked out her cute little rear and nodded. Strange how she could make him emotional one minute and humor him the next. "I suspect. Some folks do complain about their butts afterward."

She heaved herself onto the gelding. "I guess this is nothing for a former rodeo cowboy. What event did you compete in?"

He finished packing his horse. "Bareback."

"Is that where you get bucked ar   without a saddle?"

Humored once again, he grinned. Sh   was already favoring her rear, wriggling in her seat. "That's about the size of it."

"And you deliberately chose that as your profession?"

"I surely did." He watched her grimace through another city-slicker wriggle. "You could schedule a massage later," he suggested. "And soak in the whirlpool."

"Or I could tough it out like a true cowgirl." She pushed her heels down, settling into her stirrups. "Will I see you tonight, Bobby? Maybe at dinner?"

"I don't think so. I'm going to turn in early. I've got some business in San Antonio over the next few days. I'll probably be heading out before dawn."

"So when will I see you again?" she asked.

"At your party," he told her. "I won't miss your birthday, Julianne."

"Are you going to bring someone?"

He mounted his horse, tried to act casual. "No. I think I'll go alone."

"I'm always alone." When a strand of hair blew across her face, she shifted the reins to free her hand, to tuck the fiery locks behind her ear. "I haven't dated since the divorce. It's just not that easy."

He chose not to comment, not to admit that he knew how she felt.

Side by side, they started across the grass, heading for the trail back to the barn. As a stream of silence ensued, a butterfly winged by, reminding Bobby of his borrowed time with Sharon, of summer days, colorful flowers and shattered dreams.

"Maybe you could be my date for the party," Julianne said.

Bobby's pulse quickened. Suddenly he ached for what she was offering. A romantic evening with a pretty lady. Flirtatious conversation. A sip of wine. A long, lingering kiss.

He glanced her way and saw that she watched him with shy anticipation.

"Sure, I could do that," he said.

What harm was there in being her date?

In pretending, just for one night, that he was still the man he used to be.

Four

The Corral, a shabby-chic bar, presented sawdust floors, rustic oak tables, a collection of pool tables and a small bandstand. A trio of female singers belted out familiar country tunes as cocktail waitresses squeezed through the Saturday-night clientele, delivering drinks and ready smiles.

Julianne sat at a crowded table, sipping a glass of wine and looking around. Kay and Mern had invited the other Elk Ridge Ranch guests and some of the staff to her party.

Everyone was here, toasting her with well wishes. Everyone except Bobby, the man who'd promised not to miss her birthday.

Disappointed, Julianne watched the door. Was he merely late? Or had he decided not to be her date, after all?

Glancing across the room at the dance floor, she spotted Jim Robbins and his wife stomping and clapping to the music. Jim was the friendly fellow who'd startled her and Bobby on the porch that first day.

Another couple, much younger and much hipper than Jim and his wife, laughed when they all missed the same line-dance step.

She reached for her wine and glanced at the door again.

And then she saw him.

Bobby entered the bar, carrying a single white rose. She excused herself from the table and went to greet him.

For a moment they just gazed at each other.

"Happy birthday," he said, handing her the rose.

"Thank you."

"I'm sorry I'm late. I just got back from San Antonio."

"That's okay." He was here now, looking strong and stylish in a chain-stitched Western shirt, a tooled leather belt and a pair of crisp jeans. Beneath a tan-colored Stetson, he wore his hair in a single braid down the center of his back. She couldn't help but wonder how long his hair was when it was loose. Or how it would feel to run her fingers through the inky blackness.

The band took a break, leaving the bar quieter than it had been. Quiet enough for romance, Julianne thought.

What would Bobby do if she stole a kiss? If she pressed her mouth to his?

They were practically strangers. Two people barely acquainted. Yet everything about him intrigued her, stirring her interest.

Her desire.

Once again their eyes met and they gazed at each other, silence looming between them.

Julianne moistened her lips and Bobby released a choppy breath. They stood near the door, not quite blending into her party.

"I can't remember the last time a man brought me a flower," she said.

"Really?"

She nodded. "It's been years. I'm not sure how many."

He broke eye contact, cleared his throat. "When I was a kid, my paternal grandmother used to talk about the legend of the Cherokee rose."

She lowered the flower, pressing the petals against her heart. "Will you tell me about it?"

He moved a little closer, then adjusted his hat in a gesture she'd seen him do more than once. "Over a hundred and fifty years ago, the Cherokee were forced to migrate when gold was discovered on their land. The journey was called the Trail of Tears."

"I've heard of that." A snippet from a childhood history class that hadn't mattered until now.

He sighed, repeating a tale he'd obviously been weaned on. "It was a long, brutal trek. They traveled during the winter, sleeping in wagons or on the frozen ground without any means to keep warm. Nearly half of the people died from the hardship, making the women, the young mothers, weep. But the elders knew the women needed to stay strong for their children, so they called upon the One Who Lives Above to help."

As Bobby continued, Julianne kept the flower against her heart, sensing its importance.

"The One Who Lives Above created a plant to spring up everywhere a mother's tears had fallen. A white rose, with gold in the center, representing what they'd lost."

Silent, she listened, mesmerized by the emotion in his voice.

"The roses grew along the Trail of Tears, and the stickers on the stems protected these special plants from those who tried to uproot them. Soon, the women became strong once again, knowing their children would flourish in the new Cherokee Nation.''

"That's a beautiful story.''

"I always thought so, too.'' He leaned into her. "Look inside your rose, Julianne.''

She glanced down and saw a glint of gold in the center of the white bloom. "Oh, my.'' Reaching for the hidden treasure, she discovered a delicate bracelet, a simple, serpentine chain.

"Thank you, Bobby. It's perfect.'' He'd given her a piece of himself, she thought. A legend. A gift from his ancestry. "Will you help me put in on?''

He clasped the bracelet around her wrist, and she considered hugging him, pressing her body to his, breathing in his scent, losing herself in the man she wanted.

In the danger, in the excitement, of an affair.

Tonight was her only chance, the last opportunity she had to fulfill her fantasy, to summon the courage to invite him to her bed.

She'd even groomed herself for a potential seduction, for a slow, sweet, sexual night. Beneath a slim black dress, she wore thigh-high stockings, wispy panties and the see-through bustier she'd accidentally dropped at Bobby's feet nearly a week ago.

"Do you play?'' he asked.

She blinked, felt her pulse jump to her throat. "Play?''

"Pool.'' He motioned to the back of the bar. "There's a free table. Should we claim it before someone else does?''

She glanced over her shoulder, in the direction he indicated. "Truthfully, I don't play all that well. But I'm more than willing to try.''

"I can help you.''

"Okay. I'll just get my wine.'' And let her cousins know she was spending the rest of the evening with Bobby.

As he headed toward the billiards area, Julianne told Mern and Kay her news, which they saluted with thumbs-up smiles, boosting her courage.

Anxious to return to her cowboy, she joined Bobby at the pool table, where he racked the balls.

"I think you should break," he said.

Julianne shook her head. "No. You go ahead."

"I want you to do it."

"All right." She set her belongings on a nearby ledge and reached for a pool cue, chalking the end because it seemed like the right thing to do. Her knowledge of the game was more than limited.

She aimed the stick at the white ball and sent it rolling into the triangle of numbered balls, barely scattering them. "I told you I wasn't very good at this."

"That's okay. I'll rerack and you can try again. Only this time, I'll help."

And help he did. He rolled up his sleeves, critiqued the way she held the cue, and then repositioned her, giving advice she was determined to follow.

This time, she crashed through the balls, sending them in a variety of directions.

She turned to smile at him and he grinned back at her.

"Keep going," he said.

"Isn't it your turn?"

He shrugged. "We don't have to play by the rules."

"That sounds good to me." After all, this was her night to break free, to teeter on the edge. To make turning forty a wild, wondrous experience.

"Take your time," he coached.

Julianne studied the table and started to go after what she thought was a logical shot. But when she glanced up at Bobby, he shook his head.

"Try it this way instead."

As he explained where to hit the ball and what pocket it should land in, he leaned into her.

His fly bumped her rear and for a second they both froze. Julianne tried to concentrate on his direction, to stay focused on the game.

But she couldn't.

He smelled like the wind, like a warm, dark, summer night. He lowered his body, just enough to bring his face closer to hers.

"You need to imagine the cue ball touching the ball you want to pot," he said.

Because the front of his jeans were still pressed against her bottom, she wondered if he was getting aroused. His breathing was raspy, she noticed, his voice rough.

"Does that make sense to you?" he asked.

The hair on his arm tickled hers and goose bumps raced up her spine. "Yes."

"Good." He stayed right where he was, his body molded to hers. "Do you want to give it a go?"

Julianne nodded, and he moved away, but not abruptly. He took his time, running his hands down her waist and over her hips. Slowly. Gently. Almost provocatively.

He was aroused, she decided. He *had* to be.

A little dizzy, she took her shot. And made it.

Stunned, she rose to look at him. And for a moment, neither spoke. They simply smiled at each other.

Soft, flirtatious smiles.

"I just might cream you," she said.

"Really?" His smile deepened. "We'll have to see about that."

They played four games and he beat her every time. But nonetheless, Julianne gave him a run for his money, making faces at him, batting her lashes, teasing him like a teenager in heat.

He teased her right back, clearly enjoying every minute of her fortieth birthday, of the sexual innuendoes sizzling between them.

Getting creamed had taken on a whole new meaning.

"Had enough?" he asked. The rest of the partygoers, including her cousins, had left over an hour ago, leaving them alone in the quietening bar.

"Have you?" She finished the last of her wine and flicked a peanut at him.

She wasn't tipsy and neither was he, but they seemed a little drunk. Naturally intoxicated.

"I think I should take you back to the lodge and tuck you into bed."

Her heart jumped. "Oh, yeah?"

"Yeah. After all, you are an old lady. And old ladies need their sleep."

"Wanna bet?" She tossed a pretzel this time. It flew past him and landed on the pool table, sliding into a corner pocket.

They looked at each other and burst out laughing. That was the best shot she'd made all night.

A few minutes later she gathered her jacket, her purse and the rose he'd given her.

She intended to let him take her back to her room. But when he put her to bed, she was going to do her damnedest to keep him there.

Bobby parked his truck in front of the lodge and cut the engine. Julianne sat next to him, quieter than she'd been all night.

But then, the evening was nearly over and he suspected she hated to see it end. He certainly did. He couldn't recall the last time he'd had so much fun.

Flirtatious fun. Barroom fun.

He looked at Julianne and felt his groin tighten.

Sexual fun. The thrill of a man and a woman recognizing a mutual attraction and acting on it. Just a little, just enough to make them anticipate a long, lust-driven kiss.

She sighed and gazed out the windshield. "The stars are so pretty."

He glanced at the sky, but only for a second. He was more interested in gazing at her, at taking in every feminine detail. Her hair, that bewitching red mane, fell in loose waves. Curled, he supposed, with a wand or an iron or some sort of heat-activated device. Because he enjoyed watching women primp, he wondered about the glossy lipsticks, shimmering powders and scented lotions Julianne used.

"You're prettier than the stars," he said.

She turned to look at him and he realized how foolish he sounded, like a guy trying to spout poetry.

"I'm sorry. That was goofy."

"No, it wasn't." She fidgeted with the strap on her purse. "It was nice."

Bobby merely nodded. Was she waiting for him to kiss her? She seemed nervous. Sort of girlish and fluttery.

Hell, he was nervous, too. Anxious about leaning over, covering her mouth, tasting her with his tongue.

"I had a good time," he said, stalling a bit, taking a minute to ease into the kiss they both wanted.

"So did I."

She smiled and he released a shuddering breath, trapped by the softness in her voice, the hardness beneath his fly.

He was aroused. So damn aroused and trying to convince himself he could handle it.

He'd pretended half the night that the slow, intimate touches and quick, verbal foreplay hadn't been driving him crazy.

And now he was stuck with a bulging zipper.

Bobby removed his hat and tossed it into the extended cab. He would get this damn kiss over with and go home and take a cold shower.

These days, he knew how to freeze his hormones.

He met Julianne's gaze. She just sat, watching him, waiting.

Determined to do this as quickly and painlessly as possible, he leaned into her. In turn, she wet her lips and leaned into him.

Then it happened. Their mouths came together. Warm and moist.

She made a sweet, soft sound and suddenly he forgot about rushing through it. Instead he lost himself in the sensation, in the flavor of a woman.

This woman, he thought.

Sliding his hands through her hair, he deepened the kiss, let the hunger, the need, wash over him. The feeling shot through his veins and caressed his loins.

Their tongues circled, dancing like fire. He licked the inside of her mouth and she made that sound again, that soft, girlish moan.

She took his hands and moved them to the front of her dress, offering him the top button. Without thinking, he loosened it, along with two more, and lowered his head to nuzzle between her breasts.

He saw a hint of sheer lace, a small swell of cleavage. But that wasn't enough. He tugged until he found a nipple, until he was rooted, kissing and tasting.

She held him there, touching his face, watching him suckle, encouraging him to do so even harder.

U-di-le-ga, was all he could think. Heat. Sweet, sweet warmth.

A shiver racked his spine. A volcano burst in his chest, working its way down the center of his body.

If this went on much longer, they'd both be immersed in hot, boiling lava.

Or heaven help him, his seed.

Struck by that mortifying revelation, Bobby pulled back and dragged a gust of air into his lungs.

He couldn't let that happen. Not now. Not like this.

He gripped the steering wheel, damning his self-control. He was forty-two, not fourteen. And he knew better.

"What's wrong?" she asked.

"Nothing. I just...we..." He paused, took another breath. "We're behaving like a couple of kids."

"We're allowed. Besides, I'm leaving in the morning."

He gazed at the front of her rumpled dress. It would be so easy to pull her onto his lap and rub himself against her. So easy to let the volcano erupt.

"Come to my room, Bobby. Stay with me tonight."

He lifted his gaze. Oh, God. Dear God.

He wanted to. So help him, he did.

But he couldn't. If he undressed, she would see him. His cone-shaped stump and the prosthesis attached to it.

And if she didn't cringe and turn away, she would ask questions he couldn't bear to answer.

Questions about the night he'd lost his leg. The night he'd killed his wife.

"Julianne." He looked into her eyes, did his damnedest to pretend he was refusing for her sake. "It's not a good idea. You barely know me."

She blinked and grabbed the front of her dress, buttoning it hastily. "I didn't...I don't usually..." Her voice disintegrated, as fragile as a winter leaf. "You're right. I should have known better."

She reached for the door handle. He knew he should stop

her, but he let her tear off instead, rush from his truck and run into the lodge.

Realizing he'd put the burden on her, Bobby dropped his head in his hands and cursed the coward he'd become.

Julianne fumbled with the card-key and then burst into tears. Shifting her purse, her jacket and the white rose, she entered her room.

She'd embarrassed herself, inviting Bobby to her bed, putting him in a position to spurn her advances.

So he'd given her a birthday gift, flirted with her, messed around a little in the car. That didn't mean he wanted to sleep with her.

She paced the empty room for a minute, unsure of what to do, of how to combat her shame.

Finally she unbuttoned her dress and dropped the garment to the floor. Standing in front of the mirror, she studied her appearance. The sheer bustier, the thigh-high hose, the wispy panties.

Suddenly she felt foolish. And ugly. So very ugly. A forty-year-old pretending to be sexy.

She removed her shoes and sat on the edge of the bed. No wonder Bobby had turned her down. She didn't have what it took to seduce a tall, stunning cowboy. He probably had younger, prettier women falling at his feet.

A knock sounded at the door and Julianne jumped up and grabbed her robe. It must be her cousins, coming by to comfort her. No doubt they'd heard her crying.

She dried her tears and belted the robe. Mern and Kay had seen her in the bustier when she'd purchased it, but she didn't want them to know how ridiculous she looked in it now.

She opened the door and froze. Bobby stood on the other

side, but from the expression on his face, she knew he
hadn't changed his mind.

He'd come to apologize, she thought. To make excuses,
to tell her, as kindly as possible, that she was bound to find
the right lover someday. That she wouldn't be alone forever. Somehow, that was even more embarrassing.

"May I come in?" he asked.

She tightened her robe and stepped away from the door.
She had no choice but to let him say his piece. If she sent
him away, she would seem like an even bigger fool.

He walked in and glanced at her dress, which still lay
on the floor in front of the mirror.

Mortified, Julianne grabbed it and tossed it on the bed.
"Would you like to sit down?"

He shook his head and they stood for a moment, silence
stretching between them. Julianne fidgeted with the bracelet
he'd given her and then realized what she was doing.

"I'm sorry," he said.

"I understand, Bobby. You don't have to explain."

"Yes, I do."

He smoothed a hand through the front of his hair. A few
strands had come loose from the braid. Although she could
see the gray at his temples, he didn't look old. He looked
dark and masculine and much too handsome.

"This isn't your fault, Julianne."

"Yes, it is. I'm the one who asked you to be with me."

"And I'm flattered, more than you can know. But I don't
have affairs." He paused, smoothed his hair again. "I
haven't made love in over three years."

She glanced at the ring on his ringer. "Since your wife
died?"

He nodded and she couldn't help but wonder about the
woman he'd married, who she was, how he'd met her. "I

haven't been with anyone since the divorce. It's been two years for me.''

"I know. I mean, that's what I figured. You already told me you haven't dated." He jammed his hands into his pockets, blew out an audible breath. "But my situation is different from yours. Spontaneous sex, or sex in general, I suppose, is awkward for me."

"It's awkward for me, too. I married Joe when I was eighteen, fresh out of high school. He's the only lover I've ever had." And their sex life hadn't been all that great, especially at the end.

"Maybe so, but it's still not the same. I'm an amputee, Julianne. Most of my left leg is gone, and what remains of it isn't a very pretty sight."

She tried not to stare, to seem as shocked as she was. Suddenly she didn't know where to look, what to say, how to react. She'd never known anyone with a disability.

"I wear a prosthesis," he said.

Julianne nodded. Just recently she'd seen a picture in a magazine, an ad for running shoes, with a Paralympics contender wearing a metallic limb. Is that what Bobby had? Or was his prosthesis covered with some sort of plastic or simulated skin?

"I don't need adaptive equipment in my truck because I can use my right leg to brake and accelerate, the way anyone driving an automatic would do," he explained. "But I've had to make some adjustments on horseback."

"Like mounting on the opposite side?" she asked, realizing it was the first question she'd managed since he'd told her. The first words she'd spoken.

He removed his hands from his pockets. "Yeah."

"It doesn't matter," she said.

When he frowned, she wanted to kick herself. "I'm sorry. That didn't come out the way I meant it."

He shrugged. "You don't have to apologize. I know it makes people uncomfortable."

Yes, she thought. She was uncomfortable. But only because she wasn't sure if she should tell him that she still thought he was one of the most attractive men she'd ever met.

"When did it happen?" she asked.

"Three years ago. In a car accident."

Julianne closed her eyes, opened them. "Is that how your wife died?"

"Yes."

"Oh, Bobby." She started to move toward him, but he held up his hand to stop her.

"Don't do that. Don't pity me."

She swallowed the lump in her throat. "It's not pity. It's compassion."

"I didn't come here looking for compassion. And I certainly don't want to talk about my wife." He glanced at her bed. "You have the right to know why I turned you down. And that's why I'm telling you all of this."

"So you really wanted to be with me?" she asked, moving a little closer.

He shifted his gaze, allowed his eyes to meet hers. "Yes."

She took a breath, drawing courage with it. "Then be with me. Don't let tonight end without us making love."

He made a frustrated expression. "Don't you get it? I'm not comfortable taking my clothes off in front of you, Julianne."

She stood her ground. "Then don't remove them. Don't undress all the way."

He came forward, but he didn't stop until they were nearly face-to-face. "What am I supposed to do? Just shove you against the wall and unzip my pants?"

She knew he was being sarcastic, but it didn't matter. She didn't want to lose him. "You don't have to shove me anywhere. I'll go willingly."

He took her hand, pushed it against his fly. "Are you going to unzip my pants, too?"

Her fingers scraped his zipper. "If you want me to."

He made a rough, tortured sound. A masculine groan. And then he kissed her. So hard he took her breath away.

Their teeth scraped, their tongues dived. She gripped his shoulders; he cupped her bottom and rubbed her against the front of his jeans.

When he stepped back, his eyes were dark and intense. "I want to see what you have on under your robe."

Suddenly her insecurity surfaced, her fear of not being pretty enough, of trying to appear sexy. "It's the same thing I had on under my dress. The black lace."

"Show me."

"Can I dim the lights?"

"No."

"Bobby, don't be that way."

"Why not? You started this."

Fine, she thought. *Fine.* She lifted her chin and dropped her robe. "See? Black lace."

He grinned and she wanted to throw her temper at him. But she didn't. Because his grin was too damn boyish. Too damn cute for a man his age.

"I've had fantasies about that skimpy little outfit."

"You have not."

"Oh, yes, I have. Ever since it got caught under my boot." He stopped grinning. "You look incredible. More beautiful than I'd imagined."

"Really?"

Instead of responding he grabbed her and pulled her into his arms. Before she could take a breath, he attacked her bustier, tugging at the padded cups, freeing her breasts, sliding his hands down her legs, unhooking the garters.

Julianne grabbed the front of his shirt and lifted it from his pants. She bared his chest and scraped a finger down his stomach. He had a sprinkling of hair leading to his zipper.

Together, they undid his jeans. He was hard and thick and generously aroused. She stroked him, making moisture seep at the tip.

He backed her against the dresser and lifted her onto it. She opened her legs and watched him slip his hand down the front of her panties.

He rubbed her, slowly, steadily, until she pressed against his fingers and sucked his tongue into her mouth.

They both went a little crazy, kissing and licking, nibbling and biting. But Julianne didn't care. All she wanted was this moment.

This man.

When he pulled her panties down, she recalled the condoms she'd stuffed in the top drawer. But she decided not to say anything, not to bother with a hindrance that didn't matter anymore. Bobby hadn't been sexually active in years and neither had she. They didn't need protection, not even from conception.

He adjusted his jeans, pushing them down, just enough to make penetration easier. She raised her hips and as he thrust into her, they both cried out.

From the longing.

From the hunger.

From the hard, hot, mind-numbing motion.

He withdrew and entered her again, heightening the feeling, the fast, driving rhythm. She bit down on her lip and he kissed her, his tongue mimicking their lovemaking.

Desperate sex, a craving to mate. Two people who barely

knew each other, taking pleasure in the forbidden. In a one-night stand. In bumping and grinding and moaning in each other's arms.

Wetter. Harder. Deeper.

Something exploded in front of Julianne's eyes. Stars. Fireworks. A sensation so intense, she went over the edge, digging her nails into his skin.

He kept kissing her, kept thrusting deeper, pushing toward his own climax. And when it happened, he spilled into her, leaving her dizzy and breathless.

A minute passed. Then another.

They looked at each other, neither quite knowing what to say.

He stepped back and fiddled with his jeans, zipping himself back into them.

While he buttoned his shirt, she spotted her robe on the floor and reached for it. She couldn't invite him to stay, to climb into the shower with her, to cuddle until dawn.

He wouldn't strip in front of her, and she wasn't sure she wanted him to. Not now, not during this awkward lull. She wasn't ready to view his amputated leg and he wasn't ready to show her.

Nor would he ever be. After tonight, they would never see each other again.

"Are you all packed?" he asked.

She nodded. "Pretty much."

"The green suitcase?"

She managed a smile. Her lucky suitcase. "It hasn't failed me yet."

He smiled, too. "If you say so."

When he came forward, she knew he was going to kiss her. A gentle kiss. A goodbye.

Suddenly she wanted to cry. His lips touched hers, as

magical as moonlight, as tender as the rose he'd given her. She would never forget him.

"Be good," he told her.

"You, too."

He didn't offer to stop by in the morning to see her off, but she hadn't expected him to.

He reached for her hair, let it slip through his fingers. "You better get some sleep."

"I will."

She wanted to release his hair from the braid, but somehow that seemed an invasive thing to do, so she curled her fingers into his shirt instead. If only he would ask for her phone number, offer to keep in touch, make some sort of promise.

A second later he kissed her again.

And then left her room, and her life, without another word.

Five

A month later Julianne paced her apartment in Clearville, Pennsylvania. She'd been fighting a debilitating illness for nearly a week. Only now she knew it wasn't a virus or bacterial infection that had been upsetting her stomach every day.

It was a baby.

Julianne McKenzie, the woman who couldn't conceive a child, was pregnant.

"Is the doctor sure?" Kay asked.

Julianne stopped pacing to acknowledge her cousin. Kay sat on the printed sofa, wearing a pair of jeans and an oversize T-shirt. Her dark hair was clipped in a rooster-style ponytail, making her look younger than her thirty-two years.

"Yes, the doctor is sure." She'd seen him two days ago and she'd argued with him then, insisting his diagnosis was wrong, that the nurse must have mixed up her urine sample with someone else's. But a blood test indicated the same results.

She was pregnant.

Kay picked up her soda. "Has Bobby called you back?"

"No." Julianne glanced out the window. The weather was hot and muggy, stifling. "But I didn't leave urgent messages." All she'd done was give her name and phone number to the receptionist at the lodge. Twice.

"Urgent or not, he should still give you the courtesy of returning your calls."

But he hadn't, which meant he wasn't interested in talking to her. Yet she couldn't let it go. She was carrying his child and she had to tell him.

She sat next to her cousin. "I hope he doesn't think I tricked him. He is a wealthy man and I'm—" Nervous, she thought. Worried about his reaction. She couldn't bear for Bobby to think that she'd gotten pregnant on purpose, that she was trying to manipulate some money out of him.

Kay reached for hand. "Don't do this. Don't blame yourself."

"But I told him I couldn't have kids."

"You didn't lie, Jul. That's what you believed at the time."

"What if he never returns my calls? What am I supposed to do then? Fly to Texas and confront him?"

"Sounds like a plan to me."

Julianne fought the tears gathering in her eyes. "I've always wanted a baby. But why did it happen now? And why with Bobby?" A man she barely knew. A man who still wore the wedding band his dead wife had given him.

Kay squeezed her hand. "I don't know. But just think of it as God's plan. As something that was meant to be."

Would Bobby accept that reasoning? Or would he see this as Julianne's trick? Would he be angry with her? Or infuriated with himself for sleeping with her? "I should have mentioned the condoms. I should have said something."

"So you made a mistake. A judgment in error. It happens."

"But the condoms were right there. Just a few feet away." She'd even had a foil packet in her purse.

"And you considered them. Rationalized why you didn't need them."

Maybe, but that didn't alleviate her stress. Or the stress Bobby would endure. "How long should I wait for him to call me back before I head to Texas? A few days? A few weeks?"

"I'd leave another message, then opt for a few days. A few weeks are too long, Jul. You've got to get this settled before then. Besides, I know you haven't quit thinking about him."

That was true. Even before she'd discovered she was pregnant, she'd lain awake each night, recalling every moment she'd spent with him. His voice. His smile. His touch.

"I'm so scared, Kay."

"About having a baby? Or about telling Bobby?"

"Both." After all, she was a forty-year-old who'd conceived a child out of wedlock. A child with a man who haunted her dreams.

A man who hadn't even bothered to return her phone calls.

Bobby checked his watch. As usual, his nephew was late. They'd scheduled a meeting at the barn, but Bobby had gotten tired of waiting, so he'd stepped outside to watch the horses in pasture.

A man couldn't have too much money or too many

horses, he thought, admiring a young gelding he'd recently purchased.

Bobby had grown up dirt poor, first shoveling manure on other people's ranches and then breaking and training other people's horses, scrimping and saving for enough money to follow his dream. To chase the rodeo from town to town, to kick ass on the professional circuit, the way his older brother had done.

Cameron Elk, his dead brother.

Michael's wayward father.

Bobby glanced at his watch again, and when he heard footsteps, he looked up, ready to give his rebellious nephew hell for being late. The boy was too damn much like Cam.

But it wasn't Michael heading down the path that led to the barn.

It was a woman.

Her watery outline didn't spark familiarity, but even in the distance her hair looked like a fire-tinged halo, blazing in the July sun.

He knew instantly it was Julianne.

His stomach knotted with nerves, with a sexual pull he'd been trying to forget.

He started toward her, meeting her halfway.

They stopped beneath a flowering tree and stared at each other. She didn't look well. Her skin was pale and her eyes lacked their usual luster.

"What are you doing here?" he asked.

She adjusted the strap on her handbag, and he noticed the bracelet he'd given her, glinting on her wrist.

"You never returned my phone calls, Bobby."

So she came all the way to Texas? Arrived on his doorstep unannounced? "I've been busy." And avoiding her purposely. They hadn't agreed to keep in touch, to catch up on each other's lives, to pretend they would remain life-long friends. For Bobby, it was easier to lock her away in his memory.

She pushed a strand of her vibrant hair away from her ashen face. "I have something really important to discuss with you."

"Okay. I'm listening."

"Can we go someplace cooler? It's so hot out here."

He supposed it was hot, even in the shade. But he'd gotten used to being outdoors. He preferred working in the sun to being cooped up indoors.

"We can go to the barn. To the office."

"That's fine." She glanced down at the ground, released a shaky-sounding breath.

"Are you sick, Julianne?"

She lifted her gaze. "Sort of."

Once they were inside, he offered her a seat. The office he shared with Michael presented two sturdy desks, floor-to-ceiling bookshelves and a grouping of custom-crafted chairs. Bobby's desk was spotless and Michael's was a mess, cluttered with Lord knew what.

"Can I get you something to drink?" he asked. "A soda? A cup of coffee?"

Julianne folded her hands on her lap. "I'd prefer water, if that's all right."

"Sure." He went to the minifridge, removed a plastic bottle and handed it to her. She seemed tense and he wondered how serious her illness was. How could someone be sort-of sick?

She sipped the water sparingly, as if she was afraid to put too much into her stomach at once.

"What's wrong?" he asked.

She closed her eyes, opened them, then shifted her gaze to the floor. "I'm pregnant."

His hand slipped off the desk. He didn't need to ask if

the baby in question was his. If it wasn't, she wouldn't be here.

Another Elk bastard. Another illegitimate mixed blood.

Suddenly he felt like Cameron, like the irresponsible brother, the love-'em-and-leave-'em cowboy who didn't have the good sense to use a condom. "I thought you were sterile."

She blinked and he feared she might cry. She looked so damned vulnerable, so frail. Like a broken-winged fairy.

He prayed she wouldn't shatter, crumble right in front of his eyes. He could barely hold himself up, let alone keep her together. "I'm sorry. I didn't mean to sound so accusatory, but you told me you couldn't have children."

"I didn't trick you, Bobby. I didn't do this on purpose."

"I didn't say you did."

"But that's what you're thinking."

"No, it isn't." At the moment he wasn't thinking at all. His brain had gone numb. "All those years you tried to have kids and you turn up pregnant now. I don't get it."

She glanced at the floor again. "Neither do I."

Bobby went to the fridge and grabbed a water, needing to douse his anxiety, to give himself a minute to think. To breathe. To accept what was happening.

If only he *were* Cameron, if only he could turn away and say that he couldn't handle being a father, that he wasn't ready for this.

"I don't know what to do, Julianne."

"You don't have to do anything. I can raise this baby by myself."

He studied the stubborn rise of her chin, the body language that told him she intended to protect her child. To nourish it. To love it.

With or without him.

For a second he thought about Michael's mother. She'd

been dying of cancer when he'd met her, but she'd done her best to raise her son, to love him, to protect him. To do all of the things Julianne would most likely do.

But Michael's mother had suffered financially and her son had run wild.

Maybe he could offer Julianne a settlement, enough to give her and the baby a good, safe life.

That wouldn't be the same as walking out on his kid, would it?

Bobby gulped his water. Of course it would. The child would know his money, but it wouldn't know him. He wouldn't be a father, not in the true sense of the word.

He looked at Julianne, wondering about her. Where she worked, if she was content with the direction of her life. "What do you do?" he asked, realizing they'd never discussed her career. "What's your profession?"

"I'm a retail manager. And I just landed a new job. I'm supposed to start in two weeks."

"What kind of retail?"

"Women's fashion." She lifted her chin again. "The pay is the same as my last job, but the benefits are better."

He suspected she referred to medical benefits, the insurance that would provide the health care she would most certainly need.

"Why did you switch jobs?" he asked cautiously. "Was it because of the baby?"

"No. The last store I worked at closed. I was in transition when I came here last month."

And she was in transition again, he thought. Unmarried and pregnant.

He leaned against his desk. Suddenly he wanted to hold her, to make everything all right. To tell her she wasn't alone in this.

But instead he remained right where he was, guarding his emotions, his reluctance to do the right thing.

"How long will you be in Texas?"

"Three days. I'm going to get a room at the motel in town."

"You can stay here. And I don't expect you to pay the bill," he added, knowing she'd chosen the motel in town because it was considerably cheaper than the ranch. "After all, we need some time to discuss our situation. To figure it out."

"Thank you," she said before they both fell silent.

She glanced out the window and he realized that talking about their situation wasn't going to be easy. He'd never expected to see Julianne again, yet here she was, reminding him of the night they'd made fast, reckless love.

The night using protection hadn't even crossed his mind.

When the phone rang he leaped for it, grateful for the interruption.

Michael's voice came on the line. "Hey, I'm sorry I flaked on our meeting. I sort of forgot about it. But I can swing by the barn now if you want."

"No, that's okay. I've got some other business to tend to." He glanced at Julianne, wondered if she was hungry, if she needed to fill her belly. "I'll hook up with you later."

Bobby ended the call and watched Julianne sip her water. He didn't know a damn thing about expectant mothers, but he'd heard they were supposed to glow.

Well, she wasn't glowing. The woman he'd impregnated looked downright ill.

"Come on," he said. "I'll drive you to the lodge and Maria can check you into a room."

"Okay."

She gave him a halfhearted smile and guilt clawed its way to his chest. He'd been taught that a man should marry a woman if he got her in trouble. Of course, Cam hadn't followed that rule, and Bobby wouldn't, either.

He couldn't bear to take a wife. Not ever again.

Julianne stood beside Bobby at the reception desk at the lodge, fighting a bout of nausea. She had soda crackers in her purse, but she didn't want to attract attention to herself by eating in front of everyone. So she remained quiet and still, praying the queasiness would pass.

"Check again," Bobby told Maria.

The Latina woman tapped on a computer keyboard, then shook her head. "There is still nothing available until next week, Señor Bobby. *Nada.*"

He cursed beneath his breath and Julianne realized what was happening. The ranch was booked.

"I can get a room in town," she said.

He turned to look at her, his gaze settling on her still-flat stomach. "No way. That motel is a dive. I'll figure something else out."

They stood there for a moment, Bobby frowning and Julianne considering the crackers in her purse, wishing the queasiness would settle.

In the years she'd been desperate to have a baby, she used to imagine pregnancy being magical and romantic. And she'd assumed morning sickness was contained to mornings.

"You can stay at my place," Bobby said.

Stunned, Julianne blinked. Maria seemed surprised, too. She fussed behind the counter, but it seemed obvious, at least to Julianne, that the receptionist was eavesdropping.

"Thank you. That's a very generous offer." And it made her wonder why he was willing to share his home with her. He seemed so guarded, so distant, yet his offer spoke otherwise.

She glanced at the bracelet he'd given her, at the shiny gold memory.

Suddenly her stomach felt better. Calmer. She longed to be near him, to know more about him.

She hadn't forgotten Bobby and he'd become even more important now.

Because his child grew in her womb.

A child she'd already begun to love.

"I promise not to be a burden," she said.

He shrugged. "Don't worry about it. I'll bunk with Michael while you're here. He's got plenty of space."

Julianne flinched, instantly trapped in a myriad of emotions—disappointment, confusion, self-admonishment.

Bobby shouldn't matter as much as he did. Images of him shouldn't be keeping her up at night. She shouldn't care if he chose to stay with his nephew instead of with her.

Yet she did.

"Where's your bag?" he asked, steering her away from the reception desk.

"In my rental car." Her nausea returned and she gave in and reached for the crackers.

Bobby watched her for a second. "If you're hungry, I can fix something for you at my place."

"Crackers settle my stomach," she admitted, doing her best to steel her nerves, to pretend she was stronger than she felt. "Most of the time, anyway."

He shifted uncomfortably. "Then I'll have room service send some saltines to my house."

"Thank you."

He moved closer, close enough for her to smell his cologne, the warm, woodsy fragrance she recalled much too intimately.

"I'm sorry, Julianne."

"For what?" Making her pregnant? Not using a condom?

"I'm just sorry you don't feel well."

She sighed, grateful he was referring to her morning sickness. She didn't want to discuss the night she'd conceived. Not now, not while she was feeling emotional about him. "It comes with the territory. But I've been told it will pass."

"I've heard that, too." He started toward the door, paused to wait for her. "You'll have to follow me to my cabin. It's a little off the beaten path."

"That's all right."

She got behind the wheel of her rented sedan and he climbed into his truck.

The road to his cabin was narrow and rough. She jammed another cracker into her mouth and weathered the bumpy motion.

Finally they reached a primitive log dwelling, cozied on the side of a hill. The wooden structure sat on a bed of grass, surrounded by trees and a rebellious, weedy spray of wildflowers.

She exited her car and breathed in the clean, fresh scent, the beauty of the Texas Hill Country. A big, yellow butterfly winged by and she watched it flit from flower to flower.

For an instant she imagined a little boy or girl with dark hair and copper skin chasing that butterfly, running through the grass, playing in the sun.

Her child, she thought, touching her tummy. Bobby's child.

The butterfly flew away and when she turned to glance at Bobby, she caught him staring at her.

She had no idea what he was thinking. He didn't seem

angry about her pregnancy the way she'd anticipated, but he didn't seem to be settling into the idea, either.

If only he could feel the connection she felt to their unborn child. The tenderness. The love.

Self-conscious, she broke eye contact and went to the car and removed her bag.

He took the lightweight leather satchel from her. "What happened to the green suitcase?"

"I didn't feel like lugging it around. Besides, I'll only be here for a few days."

Enough time, she prayed, for Bobby to decide that he wanted to be part of their child's life. A long-distance father, a summer dad. Anything that showed he cared, that he didn't intend to abandon the baby.

He unlocked the door and ushered her inside.

The cabin reflected the man who owned it—dark and private. The walls were chinked log, the hardwood floors covered with Navajo rugs. The furniture ranged from polished antiques to homespun fabrics, and the hearth had been swept clean.

In fact, everything was amazingly clean. Spotless.

He didn't favor knickknacks, nothing that collected dust, nothing that added casual warmth. She got the saddened feeling that Bobby Elk survived rather than lived here.

"It's one bedroom, one bath." He indicated the kitchen, an open space with butcher-block counters and clay-tiled floors. "There isn't much in the fridge, but I'll make sure it gets stocked."

"Thanks, Bobby. I appreciate this."

"Sure." He placed her bag on a cowhide chair in the living room. "I should pack a few things to take with me to Michael's."

"Go ahead." Feeling like an intruder, she stepped back.

She wouldn't dare follow him into his bedroom, even though she would be sleeping there over the next few days.

While he packed, she went into the kitchen, but she didn't poke through the cabinets. Instead she sat at the small oak table and ate her crackers.

He returned within minutes and she realized that he was used to throwing his belongings together, that he'd probably lived on the road for a good portion of his life.

"Do you want to eat some real food?" he asked.

"No. Not yet." She needed to give the saltines some time to digest.

"You're going to waste away, Julianne."

She smiled, touched by his concern. "I'll be getting fat soon enough."

He looked at her stomach, then shifted his gaze back to her face. "It's so hard to fathom."

She knew he meant the baby. The life they'd created.

For a moment they watched each other, silent. Uncomfortable.

Then he went about the task of making a pot of coffee. "I don't suppose you want any."

"No, thanks. You wouldn't happen to have any tea, would you? It's easier on my stomach."

He shook his head. "No, but I'll put it on the list." He made enough coffee for one cup, poured it into a sturdy mug and drank it black.

As usual, his hair was plaited into a single braid that fell to the center of his back. His sideburns were neatly trimmed, his jaw clean-shaven.

He wore a soft, well-worn T-shirt and a pair of faded jeans. His knees were dusted with a little dirt and when she found herself looking at his legs, she quickly shifted her gaze.

There were times she forgot he was an amputee. He was

so active, so broad-shouldered and strong, it was difficult to picture him with only one leg.

"I should go. I have to hook up with Michael." He finished his coffee, rinsed the cup and placed it in the dishwasher. Next he cleaned the coffeepot, dumping the used filter in a trash can below the sink and scouring the carafe.

Julianne usually let her dishes pile up for a while before she loaded them into the dishwasher, and she didn't clean the coffeepot each time she used it. She would have to tidy up after herself while she was here, try to live the way Bobby did.

"I'll come back later."

She nodded. "Okay."

He wrote something on a tablet beside the telephone. "I'm leaving a few numbers for you. The front desk, the barn office, my cell phone. Call if you need anything."

"I will."

He left the cabin with a duffel bag slung over his shoulder and a pair of crutches in his hands.

He didn't turn back to look at her, and she sensed his discomfort. The crutches were a blatant reminder of the leg he'd lost. She supposed he needed them when he wasn't wearing his prosthesis. Why else would he have taken them, calling attention to his handicap?

Julianne just sat for a minute, staring at the walls, wondering who Bobby Elk really was.

Finally she stood and headed for his bedroom, then stopped when she saw the bed. The mahogany frame was dark and masculine, the quilt a rich shade of blue. She envisioned him sleeping there, with the windows open, stars lighting up the night.

She wanted, so desperately, to rummage through his drawers, to solve mysteries about him. Did he keep a picture of his wife anywhere? Was there a photo album tucked away?

Feeling like a thief, she gave in to her curiosity and snooped, finding nothing but neatly folded clothes. The top of his dresser held an old Louis L'Amour novel, a slightly melted candle and an abalone shell containing a bundle of a half-burned dried herb tied with red yarn. His closet didn't reveal anything but a selection of Wrangler jeans and Western shirts.

The bathroom, however, spoke of his disability. The toilet had metal rails beside it, like the safety device in handicapped stalls in public rest rooms. The tub had rails, as well, with a flexible showerhead and a waterproof chair in the center. Which, she assumed, meant that Bobby didn't shower with his prosthesis on.

Suddenly claustrophobic, Julianne rushed outside to breathe in the summer air.

She was having a baby with a man she hardly knew, a man who kept himself sheltered in a small, secluded cabin.

A place, she thought, for him to hide.

Julianne gazed at the wildflowers thriving in the sun. She knelt to pick one and within minutes she had a fragrant bouquet in her hand.

Returning to the cabin, she took the flowers with her, determined to add a spot of color to Bobby Elk's dark, isolated world.

Six

Bobby couldn't find Michael. He needed to talk this through, to confide in someone, but his nephew had taken off, Lord only knew where.

So Bobby had spent hours alone, pacing his office, knowing he didn't have any choice but to go back to Julianne.

And say what? That he was scared? That the idea of being a father petrified him?

No, he thought. Because deep down that wasn't true.

Bobby had intended to have children with his wife. He'd always thought he was meant to be a dad. But that dream had died with Sharon.

So many tangible dreams had died that day. So many joys he'd been looking forward to.

But he couldn't stop living. Not completely. It wasn't the Cherokee way.

He'd been taught to give thanks, to honor life. It wasn't

easy, not after what he'd done to Sharon, but he did his best to wake up every morning and say a Cherokee prayer.

He gazed out the window and reflected on his youth, on the spiritual lessons that still guided him.

Some Cherokees believed that an infant didn't receive a soul until it was born, but Bobby had been taught otherwise.

He believed an infant's soul entered the womb from the moment of conception. Which meant his son or daughter was already a spiritual being.

A tiny soul that was meant to be. A life he'd helped create.

Yet he was fighting its existence, practically denying his own flesh and blood.

Why? What did he have to fear?

The woman, he thought. The child's mother.

"What does Julianne expect from me?" he asked out loud, looking for answers. Did she want him to marry her? Was that why she came to Texas?

Bobby turned away from the window. He couldn't marry Julianne, not even out of duty, out of respect and honor to his child.

And that shamed him.

The baby deserved better.

But God help him, he couldn't do it. He couldn't ask Julianne to be his wife.

Maybe that wasn't what she wanted. Maybe she—

Hell. He had no idea what she wanted, and he wouldn't know until he asked her.

Fifteen minutes later Bobby returned to the cabin, stalling when he reached the porch. He couldn't just barge in, even if it was his house.

He knocked on the door, lightly at first and then a little harder.

Julianne answered with an apprehensive smile. She'd changed into a filmy dress and a pair of strappy sandals. Her hair looked freshly combed, as bright as fire and as straight as rain.

"Thank you for the groceries, Bobby. They arrived a few hours ago."

He entered the cabin. "Did you eat?"

She nodded. "I had a snack, but I'm about ready for dinner. Do you want to join me?"

"Sure." He wasn't overly hungry, but talking over a meal might be easier.

She stepped a little closer. "How about some pasta? A salad? Maybe some garlic bread?"

"Sounds good."

They headed for the kitchen and he stopped when he saw the table. She'd picked some leafy flowers and arranged them in a drinking glass.

"I looked for a vase, but I couldn't find one," she said.

"I guess I don't have one."

"I put a bouquet in the bedroom, too."

He went to the fridge, found the salad fixings. He didn't want to imagine her sleeping in his bed, sliding under his covers, resting her head on his pillow.

She opened several cans of tomato paste and started the sauce from scratch, adding fresh herbs the chef's assistant had probably gathered.

He turned and her shoulder brushed his side. Just a slight touch, a breeze, a whisper. Yet he felt it everywhere, in the center of his chest, down his stomach, beneath his zipper.

"Rigatoni?"

"What?"

"Do you want rigatoni? Or would you prefer something lighter, like angel hair?"

She looked like an angel, he thought. An Irish angel, with

flaming hair. Angel hair. Devil hair. He couldn't be sure. "Let's go for rigatoni."

Side by side, they prepared the meal. She hummed while she cooked and he realized she did so unconsciously. He supposed she would hum to the baby, too.

He glanced at her stomach, wondered if the little Cherokee was the size of a peanut. Or a walnut. Or maybe a bean.

Embryos resembled kidney beans, didn't they?

Nearly five weeks had passed since Julianne had conceived, but Bobby had no idea what was taking place in her womb.

His child already had a soul, but did it have fingers? Toes? Were tiny organs already forming? The heart? The kidneys? Or was it too soon for any of that?

Julianne probably knew. Most likely, the doctor had told her.

Determined to keep busy, Bobby worked on the salad. He opened a bag of prewashed greens and dumped the lettuce into a bowl.

Rinsing a handful of cherry tomatoes, he stole a glance at Julianne. She looked healthier than she had when she'd first arrived at the ranch, but he supposed her stomach had settled.

She started humming again, stirring the sauce with a big wooden spoon.

For a moment he just stood, watching her.

He'd heard somewhere that babies listened to outside noises from the womb, reacting to their parents' voices, recognizing them later.

It had sounded a little odd at the time, but now he wondered if it were true. There was so much he didn't know; so much he still had to learn.

Maybe he should stop by the library later and pick up a book about prenatal development.

No maybe about it. That was exactly what he was going to do. He needed to learn about his baby, to start being a father, even in the simplest way.

"Do you have a colander?" she asked, interrupting his thoughts.

He reached above the stove and removed the item she requested. She drained the pasta and completed their meal.

The garlic bread came out of the oven at the same time the rigatoni got smothered in marina sauce and, within minutes, they sat across from each other.

He glanced at the bouquet on the table, at the makeshift vase, at the simple beauty Julianne had created.

It seemed out of sync. But so did the idea of her staying in his cabin, sleeping in a bed that served him each night.

Would her perfume linger on his sheets? The fragrance he couldn't seem to forget? Violets, spun sugar and bare skin.

Before his mind delved too deeply into memories, he started a conversation, asking the questions that plagued him. "What are you going to do, Julianne? What are your plans?"

"About the baby?"

He nodded and took a bite of his salad, the marriage fear creeping back in.

She tasted her salad, too. "I'm going to need a bigger place, so when I get back home, I'll start hunting for a two-bedroom apartment." She skewered a cucumber slice. "And once I start my new job, I'll talk to my employer. I plan to work for as long as I can, but eventually I'll have to take a short maternity leave."

"None of that involves me," he pointed out.

"I can't make plans that involve you, Bobby."

"I know. But you came all the way to Texas. You must want something from me."

She glanced down at her plate, then looked up, her voice soft. Maternal. "I was hoping you'd keep in touch, that you'd come to Pennsylvania when the baby is born. And maybe come back once in a while after that."

Bobby's chest constricted. All Julianne wanted was for him to get to know their child, to visit when he could, to make routine phone calls.

Simple, caring things. Things an out-of-town father should do. Things Cam had never done with Michael.

"That's not a problem." If anything, it seemed too easy, as if it wasn't enough. "I'm going to try to be a father."

She gave him a relieved smile and Bobby froze.

He sat like a statue, like an undeserving pillar of salt. Apparently, Julianne had been unsure of him, uncertain if he would come through for their child.

He'd been worried about being guilt-tripped into marriage and she'd been worried about her baby having a long-distance dad.

God, that made him feel like a bastard.

"What about child support?" he asked. "Something to help pay for the bigger apartment and whatever else you'll need before the baby arrives."

"This isn't about money."

"Money is important, Julianne." All of it mattered, he thought. Financial, emotional and spiritual security.

"Of course it's important." She fidgeted with her salad. She still hadn't eaten the cucumber slice she'd speared. "But I'm sure your lawyer will advise you to take a paternity test before you offer any kind of support."

He frowned at her. "If you say the baby's mine, then it's mine. I'm not going to challenge you. Nor will I allow an attorney to do so."

She put her fork down and cradled her stomach, and he sensed how much his words meant to her. Clearly she needed him to trust her, to believe she was honest and forthright.

Suddenly he wanted to hold her, to guide her head to his shoulder. But he knew he couldn't. That would only remind him of the night they'd kissed.

Caressed. Made love.

Their eyes met and he inhaled a breath. Julianne was glowing, the way pregnant women were supposed to. Her skin had taken on a translucent quality, and her hair shone like magic, like crimson wine.

At this strange, mystifying moment, she was more beautiful than she had ever been.

Because of the baby, he thought. The tiny life he'd given her.

Bobby cleared his throat and reached for his water. No wonder some men boasted about making women pregnant, about the potency of their seed.

Arousal was just a heartbeat away, pounding in his loins. His fertile loins.

Once again, their gazes sought, met, mated. A look that transgressed who they'd been, what they'd become.

Strangers, lovers, expectant parents.

"You should eat," he said, pointing to her still-full plate.

"You, too," she responded.

They finished their meal in silence.

After dinner, Julianne and Bobby sat on the porch. The air was warm yet breezy and the setting sun descended behind the hills, melting into jagged cliffs and grassy shadows.

He sipped a cup of coffee and she ate a bowl of vanilla

ice cream. He'd refused dessert, but she recalled that he rarely indulged in sweets.

He was a controlled man, a man who didn't act on impulse. But he appeared to be kind, as well. After just one day, the baby had begun to matter to him. Or so it seemed. She couldn't be sure what was going on in his mind.

He turned to look at her, and she studied his features: the strong jaw and high, slanted cheekbones, the slightly aquiline nose, the firm, serious mouth.

She envisioned their child with his coloring, with his rich, copper skin and straight, dark hair.

"Did you tell anyone about the baby?" she asked.

He lifted his coffee and took a sip. "No. I wanted to tell my nephew, but he took off somewhere. Does your family know?"

"I haven't mentioned it to my parents yet. They're rather old-fashioned and I doubt they'll be particularly happy about it." She pictured her mom and dad in their proper little house, with its simple beige trim and carefully mowed lawn, worried about what the neighbors would think.

"Because you're not married?"

"Yes."

He lowered his cup, kept his eyes on hers. "My parents were traditionalists, too."

"Were?"

"They're gone now, along with everyone else. Michael is the only family I have left."

Gone. He meant dead, she realized. "Was Michael's mother your sister?"

"No." He seemed surprised by her assumption. "His father was my older brother. But Cam died a long time ago."

"Did you and Cam grow up here?" she asked. She knew so little about Bobby, about the father of her child.

Once again, he seemed surprised. And, once again, she realized she'd made the wrong assumption.

"No. This is Michael's homeland. He and his mother lived in an old farmhouse she'd inherited from her family. Michael's mother was white, a descendant from German immigrants who'd settled in the area."

She waited, hoping he would offer more information.

"Michael's mother contacted me about six months before she died. My nephew was thirteen and it was the first I'd heard of him. I didn't know my brother had a son."

Stunned, Julianne glanced at the hills, at the sky turning a dark, mottled shade of blue. "Did Cam know he had a son?"

Bobby released an audible breath. "Yes, he knew. But he didn't have anything to do with Michael. Cam wasn't the dad type." He paused, set his coffee on a small wooden table near his chair. "It wasn't an easy time. My brother was already gone and I was faced with a dying woman and a rebellious teenager."

"Did Michael's mother ask you to take care of him?"

He nodded. "She knew she was dying and she didn't have any family left. If I hadn't stepped in, Michael would have been orphaned. He would have ended up in a foster home somewhere."

Julianne glanced at her ice cream, noticed it melting in her bowl. "You keep inheriting children, don't you?"

"So it seems." He looked at her tummy, smiled a little. "But I made the one you're carrying."

Yes, she thought. He'd planted the gift in her womb, the baby she'd always dreamed about.

For a while they remained quiet. Julianne sighed and the sound melded with the moment, with the grass and the trees and the tall, leafy flowers.

"What was her name?" she asked.

"Who?"

"Michael's mother."

"Celeste."

"Was she pretty?"

"She was ill when I met her. Pale and thin."

Suddenly, Julianne's heart went out to the woman who'd died, the woman who'd asked Bobby to raise her son. "Was she in love with your bother?"

Bobby reached for his coffee. "I don't know. She met Cam at the diner where she worked. And whenever he was on his way to a rodeo in this area, he would spend the night at her house. But after she told him she was pregnant, he never came back."

Julianne imagined Celeste with blond hair and blue eyes, with a smile that had turned sad. "She must have been so lonely, waiting for him to return. Hoping and praying he would be a father to their baby."

Bobby frowned into his cup and she realized her words had hit too close to home.

She couldn't take them back, so she just sat, stirring her melting ice cream.

"I'm sorry if I made you feel bad earlier," he said. "I wasn't very nice about our baby when you first told me, but I was nervous. I guess I still am."

"Me, too," she admitted.

He lifted his gaze. "I never imagined being in this position."

She understood what he meant. He'd never imagined having a child with a woman he barely knew.

She wondered if he had intended to have children with his wife, but she couldn't bring herself to ask. Not after she'd rummaged through his cabin, looking for a photograph of the woman he'd married.

For now, it was easier talking about Celeste, focusing on her tragic tale instead of picturing Bobby with his wife.

"Does Michael still live in his mother's old farmhouse?"

"Yes, he does. You can see it from this hill."

"I don't recall seeing a house from here."

He pointed to a copse of trees. "It's that way, through the oaks. Come on, I'll show you."

He reached for her hand and when their fingers connected, her skin tingled. Suddenly she felt warm and alive, as if the sun had slid through her body and into her veins.

They walked across the grass and he guided her through a maze of old, gnarled trees. He released her hand, but the heat remained.

They stopped near the edge of the hill and in the valley below, a patriotic spray of blue flowers led to a red-and-white farmhouse.

Now Julianne would envision Bobby there tonight, while she was here, at his sequestered cabin.

How many nights since they'd made love had she thought of him? Dreamed of him? Stripped off her clothes and relived his touch, his taste, his scent?

The orgasm he'd given her.

"I'm from Oklahoma," he said.

She blinked, tried to grasp his words. "I'm sorry? What?"

"You asked earlier if Cam and I grew up around here. I told you this was Michael's homeland, but I never mentioned where Cam and I spent our childhood."

His statement settled in her brain. "Oklahoma."

He nodded.

"Were you happy there?"

"As happy as any poor Indian kid could be."

She thought about the Cherokee rose, about the legend of his ancestors. "How did you build this ranch, Bobby?

How did a poor Indian kid end up with all of this? Did you make it big in the rodeo?''

"I did all right. Better than most," he added. "But quite honestly, rodeo cowboys earn considerably less than other professional athletes, so I lived modestly and invested just about everything I made. I have a natural talent for finance, I suppose. Eventually I was able to buy income property. Not here, but in Oklahoma. By the time I was thirty, I owned quite a few apartment buildings.''

"And you sold them to buy Elk Ridge?''

"Yes, but in spite of my financial success, I wasn't ready to retire. I loved the rodeo." He shrugged, brushing away his past. "But I had a nephew to raise and I couldn't take him on the road with me. Michael needed roots. And these hills were his heart, his home.''

"Is that why you decided to build a guest ranch?''

"Yes, but the concept wasn't my idea. Celeste had weaned Michael on it. The whole kit and caboodle had been their dream." The wind blew, rustling leaves on trees, sending a few falling to the ground. "So eventually, it became mine, too.''

He gazed out at the red-and-white farmhouse. "Michael didn't see me as his savior, though. He resented me for everything. For being Cam's brother, for trying to make him respect his heritage, for disciplining him after his mother died. That kid was a serious pain in the ass.''

Julianne couldn't help but laugh. Bobby laughed, too, and the sound rose like a song.

Suddenly she wanted to kiss him, to press her mouth to his, to unbraid his hair and let it flow through her fingers.

"I should get you back to the cabin," he said. "It'll be dark soon.''

She looked at him in the waning light. This man who'd

made her pregnant. Little by little, she was learning bits and pieces about him.

They cut through the trees and reached the porch just as the sun disappeared behind the hills.

Bobby glanced at his truck and she knew he would be leaving soon.

''I forgot to give you the number of where I'll be tonight,'' he said.

''I'll get a pen and paper.'' She went inside and returned with the tablet that contained the information he'd written down earlier.

He scratched out the phone number. ''Call if you need anything.''

What she needed was him, warm and strong against her body. Just one emotional embrace, one reminder of the intimacy they'd shared.

He shifted his stance, glanced at his truck again. ''I guess I better go.''

''Okay.'' Julianne held the pen and paper, not knowing what else to say.

What would happen after she went back home? Would they struggle to make conversation on the phone? Would they drift apart until the baby was born?

He reached out and, for a moment, she thought he was going to brush her cheek or maybe slip his fingers through her hair.

But he pulled back and jammed both of his hands into his pockets.

Leaving her aching for his touch.

Seven

Bobby entered his nephew's house and seventy-five pounds of black squirming fur greeted him at the door.

He gazed at Michael's dog and chuckled. Chester was about the ugliest canine in existence. His coat was curly in spots and long and coarse in others. His snout came to a point and his eyes drooped. And those ears. Dumbo would've had a good laugh over Chester.

The mutt whined and Bobby petted him. Apparently Michael wasn't home. If he were, Chester wouldn't be bugging Bobby for attention.

He headed for the guest room, with Chester tromping beside him, his elephant ears flapping.

Bobby leaned his crutches against the wall and tossed his duffel bag on the bed. After unpacking, he placed the book he'd just acquired on the nightstand. He'd made it to the library before it closed and he intended to settle in for the night and read about his kid. He'd found a six-hundred-

and-fifty-page hardback about child development, from conception to adolescence. Which, he decided, just about covered it.

Chester leaped onto the bed and wiggled his butt. Bobby rolled his eyes and scratched the mutt's head.

"You're a pest," he said.

Chester grinned and plopped down on Bobby's pillow. What the hell? he thought as he continued a conversation with the dog.

"Guess what? I'm going to be a dad." He picked up the book and found the page that had caught his attention at the library. He showed Chester a picture of a five-week-old embryo. "That's what my kid looks like. For now, anyway."

The mutt cocked his head and woofed, as if to ask who Bobby had made it with. Even the dog knew he'd been living like a monk.

"She's a redhead and her name is Julianne. She came here for her fortieth birthday." He paused and then added, "We were only together once. But she got pregnant just the same."

Chester panted excitedly, and Bobby realized he'd told the mutt too much.

"Yeah, I know. You like redheads, too." The dog was forever running off to a nearby ranch, where an Irish setter peddled her wares.

He gave Chester a serious study and tried not to wince. Thank goodness Michael had neutered him. Chester's offspring would probably look like the hind end of a baboon.

Preparing to relax, Bobby stripped down to his boxer shorts and removed his prosthesis. He usually gimped around on his crutches in the evening, as he put in long hours and often needed a break by the time his workday ended. He knew how much stress his residual limb could tolerate and he rarely pushed himself beyond those limits.

He headed for the bathroom and washed his residual limb, wiping away the sweat from the day. It perspired inside the socket, as any body part would that was encased in plastic. Next he cleaned the prosthesis with alcohol, taking care to sanitize it properly.

When he returned to the bedroom, he scooted onto the bed and glanced at Chester. The dog was still mulling over the book, probably thinking the image resembling Bobby's kid wasn't any cuter than his own pups would be.

The five-week-old embryo did look a bit like a kidney bean, with a big head and a little tail. But according to the text, its tiny heart was already beating.

Wow. How amazing was that?

He shifted his gaze to the next photo, a seven-week-old embryo. At that point, the eyes, nose, digestive system and even the first stage of toe formation was visible.

And finally, at eight weeks, the one-and-a-half-inch organism was clearly recognizable as a human fetus.

Bobby set the book on his lap, awed by the changes that would take place in Julianne's womb.

Suddenly he couldn't wait for the next few weeks to pass, to know his kid was a full-fledged fetus.

A bit too anxious for his own good, he thought about the expectant mother and wondered what she was doing.

He stole a glance at the phone. He could call her, he supposed. Just to make sure she was all right.

"What do you think?" he asked Chester.

The dog gave him a big, sappy grin.

"Okay. You talked me into it."

He dialed the number and it rang and rang. Then rang some more. Any minute, the answering machine would pick up.

Damn it. Where was she? What if something was wrong?

Just as he started to panic, Julianne's breathy voice came on the line. "Hello?"

"What took you so long? Are you okay?"

"Bobby?" she asked, obviously surprised to hear from him. "Is that you?"

"Of course, it's me. Are you sick?"

"No. I just got out of the shower. And I'm..."

Naked and wet, he thought, deciding this call wasn't such a good idea after all. Now he had a mental image.

Damp hair. Fragrant skin. A line of water trailing down her body, clinging to her navel.

"I should let you go," he said.

"No. Wait."

He heard a rustling sound and assumed she was wrapping herself in a robe. He tried to cover her up in his mind.

And failed.

So he tried again, telling himself there was nothing sexy about her showering in his tub. Not with the handicapped equipment in it.

Then again, she was naked in the same place he got naked. Had she used his soap? Slid the sudsy bar over her breasts, down her tummy, between her legs?

"Why did you call?" she asked.

Bobby's brain went blank.

Chester nudged him, calling his attention to the book. To the baby.

He snapped into the daddy focus. "I just wanted to see how you were doing. If you two were settling in all right."

"Two?"

"You and the baby."

"We're fine," she said with a smile in her voice.

He smiled, too. Then couldn't come up with another thing to say.

Silence stretched the line like a gaping hole.

Bobby stammered, trying to fill it. "So..."

So he was an idiot—a tough, old, one-legged cowboy rendered speechless by a pregnant lady.

"I should let you get back to putting on your pajamas or whatever you were planning on doing," he finally said, trying to find a dignified way to end the call.

"I am a little tired. But that's normal."

Because of the baby, he thought. "Then sleep tight and I'll see you tomorrow sometime."

"Okay. Good night, Bobby."

"'Night." He hung up, feeling stupid and mushy.

Not knowing what else to do, he picked up the book and resumed his studies, scanning information about the second trimester—the fourth, fifth and sixth months of pregnancy.

During this period, he read, women felt the first flutter of life. A soft, light movement, like the wings of a butterfly. Then later, little kicks and jabs.

He grinned, trying to imagine what that must be like. Now he was even more anxious for time to pass.

Time that didn't include him, he realized. In three or four months he wouldn't be able to put his hand on Julianne's tummy and feel one of those tiny kicks. Not if she went back home and he remained in Texas.

He frowned, wondering how many trips to Pennsylvania he would have to make to experience the advances in Julianne's pregnancy.

Too many, he thought.

And what about after the baby was born? The time factor would become even more crucial then. If he wasn't there on a daily basis, the child wouldn't bond with him. He would miss everything—the first time the baby lifted its head, smiled, crawled, walked, started school.

This baby was his destiny, a little Cherokee soul he'd helped create. Yet the child would barely know him.

He muttered a frustrated curse and Chester perked his gigantic ears.

"What am I going to do?" he asked the dog.

Chester gave him a befuddled look and Bobby cursed again.

He wanted to be a full-time dad. He wanted to raise his son or daughter, to be a strong, steady influence in the child's life.

Which meant he had to convince Julianne to stay in Texas.

For the next eighteen or so years.

Dear God. He closed the book. He had to think of something, anything, that would keep Julianne nearby.

Anything, he added, glancing at the gold band on his finger, except a marriage proposal.

The following day Julianne arrived at the barn. She entered the building and checked the office, but Bobby wasn't there. Strange, considering this meeting had been his idea.

She started down a row of box stalls, looking for him. Some of the horses whinnied and she smiled, feeling as if she were being rewarded with equine catcalls.

She stopped in front of Caballero's stall. The gelding came forward and poked his head over the door.

"Hi, there." She stroked his nose, wondering if he remembered her. "I brought you something." She reached into her pocket and removed a carrot. He sniffed her hand and snatched up the treat, munching noisily.

"Julianne," a familiar voice said from behind her.

She turned and saw Bobby, then stood like an imbecile, just staring at him, thinking how rugged he looked.

A slightly battered hat shielded his eyes and his clothes

and boots wore a thin layer of dust. A hardworking rancher in his prime, with sweat beading his brow.

"Hi," she said.

"Hi, yourself."

He smiled, and their conversation faltered. Just as it had last night on the phone. Only she had been half-naked then.

"Where were you?" she asked, trying to gain control of her senses. She could feel Caballero breathing into her hair.

"In the tack room, returning some equipment." He glanced down at his dusty clothes. "I've been working with a new gelding. He's still a little green."

"Did he kick some dirt at you?"

"More or less." Bobby lifted his gaze. "Are you hungry?"

How could a sweat-dappled man look so appealing? So touchable? "Not really. I made an omelette about an hour ago."

"Do you mind if I eat? I haven't had lunch."

"No, go right ahead."

They headed to his office, quiet again.

Bobby washed his hands in the adjoining bathroom and returned within minutes.

Julianne waited while he opened the bar-size fridge, scanned the contents and grabbed a plastic container.

He popped the lid and put the container in the microwave. Soon the room smelled heavenly.

"What is that?"

"Just a simple stew. I threw it together last night. After I talked to you," he added, without looking up. "I was restless. I needed something to do."

"So you prepared lunch for the next day?"

"I was restless," he said again. "Did you sleep okay?"

She'd fallen asleep last night in his bed, cradling his pillow, whispering a lullaby to his baby. "Yes."

"Good."

The microwave timer sounded and he removed the stew. "Are you sure you don't want some?"

He met her gaze and her heartbeat accelerated. His bed. His pillow. His baby.

"Julianne?" he asked when she didn't answer.

She touched her tummy. Was she getting sentimental over him because of the pregnancy? Because her hormones were out of whack?

"Maybe just a little," she said.

He spooned their lunch into two large mugs, filling hers halfway. Next he grabbed a bag of potato chips and two lemon-lime sodas.

"Why don't we eat outside? On the bench out front." He reached for the hot mugs, inviting her to carry the rest of their bounty.

They ate in silence for a while. The stew he'd made was rich and hearty, with big chunks of beef. The drink tasted good, too. Cool and bubbly.

"I want you to move to Elk Ridge, Julianne."

She nearly dropped her mug.

"I know this seems rather sudden, but it hit me last night. If we don't live near each other, I'll miss out on being a dad. A true dad."

She didn't know how to respond, how to react. So she just sat, stunned into silence.

"I was up most of the night, thinking it over," he said. "I can't relocate to Pennsylvania. I've got a ranch to run, so I figured maybe you could come here."

She found her voice. "And do what? I have a job waiting for me. Friends, family. I can't just pick up and leave."

"I'll make it worth your while."

She blinked, sucked in a breath. She had no idea where this was going. What he truly had in mind. Last night on the phone, he'd seemed affectionate. Attentive. Awkwardly sexual.

And now he appeared to be making a business proposition.

"You won't have to pay rent," he said. "You can live in a guest cabin. The one closest to the lodge is the biggest. The most convenient."

He paused, and something clouded his eyes. Something dark, she thought. Something haunted.

"If you don't like how it's furnished, you can redecorate. However you choose." He opened the potato chips, making too much noise with the bag, almost as if he meant to distract himself, to shake away the emotion. "I also have the perfect job for you."

She was still focused on the cloudiness in his eyes, the emotion he tried to hide. He confused her. Mesmerized her. Made her long to unravel his secrets.

"Don't you want to know what it is?" he asked.

"I'm sorry. What?"

"The job I'm prepared to offer you. Aren't you curious about it?"

"Yes, of course."

"There's an empty space at the lodge, next to the gift shop. Michael and I have been thinking about putting a Western boutique there, a place with some fancy, upscale garb. And since you're in retail, I thought you could help us get it off the ground." He turned to look at her. "This project has been on the back burner for quite a while. We've just been too busy to deal with it."

She sipped her drink and waited for him to continue. His eyes had shifted, the darkness gone.

"We'd considered leasing the space to an outside vendor, but the idea of losing creative control didn't sit well.

We prefer to own the shop ourselves and hire someone to run it.''

"And now you're offering me the job?"

He nodded. "I'm prepared to pay you what you feel you're worth.''

Overwhelmed, she took a deep breath.

"Do you like it here?" he asked. "Do you like the ranch?''

She scanned the scene in front of her, the corrals, the grassy paths, the shady trees. "Yes. It's beautiful.'' Especially the distant hills and the flower-dotted meadows. "But this isn't a decision to be taken lightly.''

And she was a little lost, a little confused. Why had he come up with this scheme so suddenly? So abruptly? She almost felt as if she were being bribed.

"What triggered this, Bobby?"

"Truthfully?'' He placed his half-eaten stew on the ground. "I checked out a child-development book from the library and the stuff I read was amazing. It made me want to experience everything. The pregnancy, the birth, the first time the baby crawls.'' He paused and grinned. "Did you know kids sometimes crawl backward in the beginning?''

His eyes had shifted again, only this time they were bright and warm. Fatherly.

Everything inside her went soft. Bobby had begun to love their baby. He felt the same connection, the same tender affection, she felt for it.

She touched her tummy, letting her hand linger. "I wasn't expecting this.'' And now she had to consider making a life-altering change. The baby deserved to have two full-time parents, two people who cared, two people devoted to its well-being.

But could she live here? So far from home?

And what about her relationship with Bobby?

Wouldn't it be awkward, seeing him every day? Fantasizing about him? Wanting him?

Or would time dissolve the attraction? Releasing her from those uncomfortable bonds?

"I don't know," she said, thinking out loud. "I don't know if it's a good idea." What if her feelings for him developed? What if they got stronger?

"Why?" he asked. "Why isn't it a good idea?"

"Because of us," she responded, trying to explain without baring her fears. "Half the time we don't even know what to say to each other."

"So we'll get past that. We can try to be better friends. We can work on it."

Friends raising a child together. It sounded simple. And complicated.

Julianne closed her eyes. A gentle breeze blew, stirring scents from earth, from the ranch that could become her home. Hay and horses and the blades of summer grass filled her senses.

When she opened her eyes, she found Bobby watching her with a strong, candid gaze. He made no attempt to hide his emotions, the enormity of what he wanted.

The desire to give their child his heart.

"Will you think about my offer?" he asked.

"Yes," she said.

"Will you come up with a decision in the next day or so? Before you leave?"

"Yes," she said again. Somehow she would.

Bobby had been waiting, worrying and wondering what Julianne's choice would be. Finally on the last day he went to the cabin. Up to this point he'd left her alone, but he couldn't wait any longer. She was scheduled to return to Pennsylvania tonight.

Would she come back? Or was he destined to be a long-distance dad?

He knocked on the door and, after a few moments, she answered.

"Bobby." She started smoothing her hair, fussing with her sleep-tousled appearance. She was still in her pajamas, a silky top and matching drawstring bottoms. "I was going to call you later."

How much later? It was already noon. "I'm sorry, but I was getting impatient."

"That's okay."

She stepped away from the door and he entered the cabin. When she started fussing with her hair again, he studied her.

The green pajamas matched her eyes, but she looked tired. Freckles stood out against pale skin like misplaced fairy dust.

Suddenly he realized noon was early for her. She was probably battling the aftermath of morning sickness.

Now he wanted to hold her, to rock her and the baby back to sleep.

"Would you like some tea?" she asked. "I was just making myself a cup."

Because the urge to hold her unnerved him, he shoved his hands into his pockets. "No thanks." He could see the outline of her breasts, the indentation of her waist.

Soon, he knew, her stomach would swell and her breasts would grow fuller, the nipples turning a darker shade of pink.

"Coffee?"

He shook his head and sat on his own sofa, waiting for her to finish preparing her tea.

Julianne went into the kitchen and then returned with a stoneware cup.

So he was fixated on the changes her body would go through. That was normal, wasn't it?

She sat in a rough-hewn chair, looking far too delicate for the dark, routed wood.

Now he wanted to hold her again, to protect her.

"I'll move here," she said.

A wave of relief flooded his body and he smiled. She smiled, too. But it seemed shaky at best, as if she were nervous about her decision.

"I have some conditions, Bobby. Some things I think we should discuss."

"I'm listening."

"I don't want to feel like I'm being kept. The free cabin doesn't work for me. I'll pay rent, the way any other tenant would."

Feminine pride, he thought, noting the tilt of her chin. He hadn't expected that.

"What about the job?"

She tasted her tea. "It interests me. I think it's a wonderful opportunity."

"Good."

"There's more."

"All right." He leaned forward. He sensed this was the part making her nervous, the condition keeping her awake at night.

"I agree that we should concentrate on being friends. But if things don't work out, I want the option to go back home."

His chest tightened. "I'm on probation?"

"No. That's not how I mean it." Her voice turned soft. "I'm really happy that you want to help raise the baby, and that's why I'm willing to move here. But I can't guarantee this situation will work. It's such a monumental change."

And she was apprehensive. Because of their awkward relationship, he decided. Because of the one-night stand neither of them could seem to forget. "It will take some time, Julianne."

"I know. But I just want you to understand how I feel."

He merely nodded. Their situation *had* to work. The child needed them. Both of them.

He summoned a smile. "We're going to be great parents."

She smiled, too. And when she drew her legs up, the cropped pajama top rode a little higher.

He wondered when it would be appropriate to touch her tummy. When he could ask without it seeming sexual.

"What should I do about my car?"

He cleared his throat. "Your car?"

"I can't drive it to Texas. I don't want to tackle a trip like that. Not by myself."

Of course not, he thought, realizing they had details to discuss. "I'll hire a company to transport your car. I'll arrange for the moving van, as well."

"Thank you. I don't intend to bring much. I'll probably put most of my furniture in storage." She paused and glanced around his cabin, as if envisioning the one she would be living in. "I want to get settled first."

"That makes sense. You can always send for things later." He glanced around the room, too. "I'm sorry I can't show you the place you'll be living in. It's still being occupied."

"That's all right."

Should he tell her more about the cabin that was to become her home? Or should he wait until she moved in?

He would wait, he decided. And then he would mention it casually. He didn't want her to know how much emotional effort it took for him to invite her to stay in his old house.

The bright, roomy cabin he had shared with his wife.

"Do you have someone to help you pack?" he asked when he caught her watching him.

She nodded. "My cousins."

"How long will it be before you come back, Julianne?"

"A few weeks. Maybe a little longer. I'll call you when I'm sure."

"Okay."

They talked for a while longer and, finally, he rose, knowing it was time to leave.

She came to her feet and walked him to the door. When she glanced up at him, his heart went soft. She still looked a little pale. Tired yet somehow pretty.

"Thank you," he said.

"For agreeing to move here?"

He nodded. "And for choosing to have my child."

She took a breath, wrapped her arms around her middle. "I've always wanted a baby."

"I know. But I'm still grateful."

"You're welcome, Bobby," she said after a beat of silence.

He met her gaze and they stared at each other, the uncertainty of their future stretching between them.

"I'll keep in touch," he told her.

"Me, too."

He walked out onto the porch, anxious for her to return to Texas.

And, God willing, to stay.

Eight

Three weeks had passed, but Julianne was still in Pennsylvania.

She looked around her bedroom and sighed. Between fighting bouts of morning sickness and a cold she'd contracted, she'd barely made a dent in packing.

Boxes, in all shapes and sizes, littered the floor. Even with her cousins's help, deciding what to ship to Texas and what to store wasn't an easy task.

But then, none of this was easy. She was moving away from everything familiar. She'd grown up in Clearville. This tiny town was all she knew.

And now there was Bobby.

He called a few times a week. Their conversations were a little shy, a little quiet, but they were sort of sexy, too.

She touched her tummy, felt her heartbeat quicken. He asked about changes in her body, and when she answered his questions, she sometimes visualized him, his shirt untucked, his jeans unzipped.

Julianne reached for a medium-size box she'd just packed and labeled it. Then she glanced at the clock: 11:00 p.m. It was earlier in Texas, but only by an hour.

Was Bobby getting ready for bed? Had he showered yet?

She could call him. She could climb under the covers and listen to his voice.

Was fantasizing on the phone wrong? Or was it a safe way to relieve the tension? To get him out of her system before she moved to Texas?

Her fear of living at Elk Ridge still weighed heavily on her mind. If her desire for Bobby escalated, she would get trapped in a sexually charged situation, wanting him every moment of the day.

Which wouldn't do her a bit of good when she was waddling around in maternity clothes with a swollen belly and fat ankles.

So call him, she thought. Get wild on the phone, and then settle down in Texas like a good little pregnant girl.

She removed her pajama bottoms and climbed into bed, wearing only the silky top and a pair of cotton panties. Should she turn down the light? Make the room more romantic?

Maybe just a little. She dimmed the three-way bulb and took a deep breath.

And then she dialed Bobby's number.

"Hello?"

He answered on the third ring and she stalled, debating whether or not to hang up, to let this foolish fantasy go.

"Hello?" he said again.

"Hi." Her voice came out in a near whisper.

"Julianne?" His voice softened, too. "You sound sleepy."

She inhaled another breath. "I'm in bed. But I just wanted to call to…"

To…

"To what?" he asked.

Good heavens. What was she going to say? She didn't know how to do this.

"Nothing," she told him, chickening out.

"You called for nothing." His tone grew stronger, deeper. "What's going on?"

She pulled the sheet to her chin. "My hormones are messed up."

"You're pregnant. That's normal."

Normal? What did he know?

"I called you to have phone sex," she blurted, afraid she might cry. Or scream. Or curl into a ball and die.

He cleared his throat, coughed, then cleared his throat again. "Really? I mean…*that's* why you called?" He paused, coughed again.

The man couldn't quit choking and she was half naked and feeling like an idiot.

Should she hang up? Say "I'm sorry"? Apologize for being flighty and emotional?

"Have you ever done it before?" he asked suddenly.

She dropped the sheet, felt her pulse pound. "No. Have you?"

"No." He cleared his throat again. "Do you want to go first?"

Julianne reached for her pillow. "Go first?"

"Start the foreplay."

A shiver crept up her spine. Say something naughty? Just out of the blue? With him waiting? "I don't think I can." She sucked in her bottom lip, tasted her own saliva. "Maybe you should go first."

''Me?'' His breath rushed out. ''I'm not very good at this kind of thing.''

Julianne sat up. ''Then maybe we shouldn't do it. Maybe we should just have a normal conversation instead.''

He made a gulping sound and she knew he'd gone to the kitchen to guzzle some water. Or possibly a beer.

''Okay,'' he said, swallowing. Hard. Much too hard. ''But I can't think of anything to talk about right now. Can you?''

''No.'' She turned the light back up. Was his shirt unbuttoned? Were his jeans undone?

He took another drink and she knew it was beer. She could hear him sucking on the bottle, slaking his thirst as quickly as possible.

''I was packing,'' she said finally.

''Oh. Is your cold better?''

''Yes, it's completely gone.''

''How's our baby?''

''Fine. I think my tummy's getting bigger.'' And so were her breasts. Already they were sore, her nipples hard and achy.

''I can't wait until you get here. I want to see you, Julianne.''

''I want to see you, too.'' She pictured him dark and handsome, looking the way she remembered him, with his hair plaited into a single braid.

''Is it warm there?'' he asked.

''Yes.'' Suddenly her pulse pounded again. Everywhere. At her wrists, against the side of her neck, between her legs. ''It's sort of hot and sticky.''

''Here, too,'' he said.

Julianne closed her eyes and Bobby drank his beer again. She could hear him swallowing, tasting the liquid, letting it slide down his throat.

Aroused, she held the phone closer to her ear and then imagined rubbing it against her pulse, against the pounding between her legs.

She wanted Bobby there, hard and thick. Hot and sticky.

"Julianne?"

"Yes?"

"I want you to come."

She opened her eyes, nearly lost her breath. "Come?"

"To Texas. Soon."

She loosened her grip on the phone, smiled a little. He knew exactly how to play this game. "You're an evil man, Bobby Elk."

He had the gall to groan. "I didn't say that on purpose."

"Yes, you did." And she adored him for it. He'd broken the tension—for both of them. "I think we should hang up and pretend this never happened."

"So your hormones are okay now?"

"Yes."

"Are you sure? Because if you want to mess around some more, we could have cyber sex." He lowered his voice. "You have an e-mail address, don't you?"

Oh, she thought, glancing at her computer. It was tempting.

"Good night, Bobby."

"'Night, pretty mommy. You sleep tight."

"I will." She ended the call, anxious to return to Texas and be friends with the father of her baby.

Warm, tender, flirtatious friends.

On the day Julianne arrived in Texas, her heart wouldn't quit pounding. Bobby had picked her up at the airport, and now they drove back to the ranch, nearing their destination.

Her new home.

Bobby glanced her way, then turned back to the road. "You look good, Julianne."

"Thank you. So do you." Better than good. He wasn't wearing a hat and she was graced with an unobstructed view of his profile—the tiny lines near his eyes, the distinguished gray at his temples.

She hadn't forgotten how handsome he was, but seeing him again—in the flesh—made her want to touch him.

Which, she knew, wouldn't be a smart thing to do. Not now. Not this soon.

Maybe later today she could hold his hand or give him a platonic hug. Later, when her heart quit pounding.

They'd greeted each other at the airport with genuine smiles, but they hadn't embraced. And now she wondered if Bobby was nervous, too.

He turned onto a long, country road that led to Elk Ridge. Trees lined the path and shrubs bloomed with color. The hills, the power of the Texas Hill Country, rose in the distance.

"It's so pretty here," she said.

He nodded. "I used to camp in hills all the time. Sleep beneath the stars."

"Used to?"

He shrugged. "I still do, just not as often."

Because it required more effort, she realized. The loss of his leg had taken some of the ease from his life, some of the simplicity.

"I've never been camping," she said.

Bobby shot her a surprised look. "Never?"

"Nope."

"Not once in forty years?"

She laughed. "No. And thank you for reminding me how old I am."

He laughed, too. "Hey, I'm in my forties, too. Remember?"

Because she got a sudden urge to stroke the gray in his hair, she folded her hands on her lap. "It's easier for men. They age better."

"Says who?"

"Everyone. It's a known fact."

"That's a load of crap." He braked at a stop sign and waited for a flatbed pickup, transporting bales of hay, to pass. "Men and women age the same. And in my culture, we honor our elders. There's nothing shameful about growing old."

Tell that to the media, she thought. To the advertising moguls who promoted youth and beauty. "You didn't like turning forty. At least that's what you told me before."

He started across the empty intersection. "I was going through a rough time. It wasn't getting old that bothered me."

Suddenly it hit her. His wife had probably died near his fortieth birthday. "I'm sorry, Bobby."

"We all go through rough times."

He shrugged off his pain, a little too easily, and she sensed his wife was still a guarded subject.

Maybe in time, he would open up and share his feelings. Wasn't that what true friendships were based on? Honesty? Emotion? Long, quiet hours of heartfelt talks?

"My grandmother lived to be ninety-three," he said, pulling her back into their earlier conversation.

"Really? And here I am, griping about being forty. Maybe if I were Cherokee, I'd have some pride in the aging process."

"You've got some Cherokee blood in you," he said.

She gave him a perplexed look. "I do?"

"Yeah." He grinned and motioned to her lap. "You're carrying my kid, aren't you?"

She smiled and touched her stomach. "Yes, I am."

And that was why she was here, moving to Texas, starting a new life.

Within ten minutes they reached Elk Ridge Ranch. He steered the truck past the lodge, took another small road and parked in front of an impressive cabin.

The windows were tall and paned, trimmed with flower boxes overflowing with summer blooms. A jutting redwood deck offered a stone hearth for outdoor warmth and cozy table to enjoy the elements.

Julianne couldn't wait to see the interior. "This is beautiful, Bobby." A cabin that appeared to be transformed into a homestead.

He unlocked the door and they stepped inside.

Cathedral-like ceilings arched in a wooden dome and sunlight spilled across hardwood floors. The living room presented Aztec prints and lodgepole pine furnishings.

She headed for the kitchen and found an equal dose of charm. Copper pots, modern appliances and bold, bright colors were mixed with warm, rustic woods.

She turned and saw Bobby standing behind her.

"I assume you like it," he said.

Like it? She loved it. "I can't believe I'm going to live here."

"There are three bedrooms, two baths, a den, a breakfast nook and a formal dining room." He motioned to the back door. "The mudroom is that way."

"I'm overwhelmed. What's in here?" She peeked into a small room off the kitchen and discovered a pantry with a long counter and a small sink.

"This was originally built for drying herbs," Bobby said as he followed her into the tidy workspace.

"It's perfect. I can dry flowers. I can make my own potpourri." She smiled at him. "I dried the Cherokee rose." Like a crush-crazed teenager, she'd kept it as a memento, a reminder of the man who'd given it to her.

"You wear the bracelet, too," he remarked, glancing at her wrist.

"Yes." Julianne fingered the slim gold chain. She never took it off. "It suits me. And so does this cabin." She went back to the kitchen and leaned against a butcher-block isle. "This is some guest accommodation."

Bobby merely shrugged. "It used to be my house."

"Your house?" She tried to contain the shock jarring her bones. "When?"

"I had this cabin built soon after Michael turned eighteen. I lived in his farmhouse when I was raising him, but he wasn't a minor anymore." Bobby paused, hooked his thumbs on the waistband of his jeans. "He was an adult, and he was bringing girls home to spend the night. Staying with him was getting awkward."

"Were you married then?"

"No."

"So you met your wife later? After you built this place?"

"Yes."

"And now you live somewhere else," she said, pressing him for more information than he seemed inclined to give.

"After my wife died, I burned her belongings and moved to a smaller cabin."

Julianne's breath hitched. "You burned—"

"It's the traditional Cherokee way," he explained before she could finish. He gazed past her. "Most of this furniture is mine. Or it was. I decided to leave it here."

"So for the past three years, your former home has been used as a rental for the ranch?"

"It's no big deal."

But it was, she thought. He'd exchanged a bright, airy house for darkness and seclusion. "Did you build the cabin you live in now?"

"Yes, but not for me, specifically. All of the guest cabins are somewhat remote. The folks who rent them are looking for an escape from the city."

"And those who want luxury stay at the lodge," she added. "Or they stay here."

"Exactly. But this place is yours now, Julianne. Yours and the baby's."

"I'll take good care of it," she said, wondering about Bobby's wife, the lady who'd lived here before her.

"How long were you married?" she asked.

"A year."

"Was she Cherokee?"

"Yes," he answered without blinking. His eyes were shielded, his feelings hidden. "She was."

Suddenly, Julianne envied his wife—the woman who'd shared his culture, his name, his heart.

Dear God, she thought. She envied a dead woman?

"Do you want to see the rest of the house?" he asked, changing the subject.

"Okay." She knew her voice was quiet, but she couldn't help the emotion crowding her soul. Bobby had burned his wife's belongings and moved out of his home, yet he continued to wear a gold band on his finger.

A ring that still made him seem married.

A few minutes later he showed her the den, where most of the boxes she'd shipped were being stored.

"I'll help you unpack," he said. "But I'm sure you'd like to rest. We can get to it later."

"That's fine."

When they entered a large, artfully decorated guest room,

Bobby gestured broadly. "This can be the nursery. We can ditch all this stuff and start over."

Julianne turned to look at him and he brushed her hand.

"This baby means everything to me," he said.

"I know." And she knew how difficult it was for him to come back to this house, to air out his memories and start new ones.

But he'd done it.

For the sake of their child.

Bobby helped Julianne unpack the following day. Most of her belongings were personal items. She hadn't shipped a lot of household goods, but he'd told her ahead of time that the cabin was stocked with necessities.

They worked in the master bedroom. He transferred her clothes from wardrobe boxes into the closet and she folded pajamas and whatnots into dresser drawers.

Whatnots?

Just say it, he told himself. Just admit that she was tucking away her bras and panties, pretty little things that kept catching his eye.

Like the garter-belt number she'd worn on her birthday. The silk and lace he'd hastily stripped from her body.

"This is a beautiful bed."

He spun around. "What?"

"The bed."

"What about it?"

"It's beautiful," she said again, motioning to the four-poster frame.

"I've never slept in it," he responded, letting her know it wasn't the bed he'd shared with his wife. "It's not part of my original furniture."

"I wasn't wondering about that. I just..." Her words drifted and she reached for her soda and took a sip.

"Thought it was nice," she added, even though they both knew she was downplaying her curiosity, pretending that her interest in the bed had nothing to do with him.

A lull of silence hit the room and he wished these awkward moments would quit happening.

Their eyes met and held, but neither of them could think of anything to say.

Damn, he thought, grimacing. Damn. Damn. Damn.

"I'm sorry," she finally said after another long, clock-ticking strain of silence. "I didn't mean to make you uncomfortable."

"You didn't," he lied.

"Oh. Okay. Well, good." She gave him a small, nervous smile, her dimple appearing for a millisecond.

When she fidgeted with her soda, he wanted to coax her to smile again. Just to see the dimple reappear. Somehow that sweet little indentation never failed to ignite his blood.

Because he'd yet to taste it.

Which was something he had no business even thinking about.

He shifted his stance. Why not? Thinking and doing weren't the same thing, and he had every right to fantasize. Especially after she'd called him for phone sex. A guy couldn't just forget something like that.

Could he?

"Do you want some?" she asked, extending her soda.

Did he want put his mouth where hers had been? Touch the lipstick mark she'd made?

Hell, yes. Definitely. You bet. He'd suck on the can if it would curb his sexual urges.

"No, thanks," he said. A few sips of cherry cola weren't going to curb a damn thing.

Julianne drank the fizzy liquid instead and he watched her, studying the woman carrying his child.

Her vibrant hair was pulled into a messy ponytail and she wore jeans and a green-and-white T-shirt—a simple, wholesome outfit that made her look younger than forty.

He supposed that would please her, considering how wrapped up in her age she was.

He cocked his head, studying her from another angle, gliding his gaze up and down her body, then settling on her waist. She didn't look pregnant. To him, her stomach still appeared flat.

"You said your tummy was getting bigger."

She glanced down, then back up again. "It is."

"Are you sure?"

"Yes, but I don't think it's the baby. I did at first, but it's too soon. I shouldn't be showing this early." She paused, made a funny face. "I think it's from all my food cravings."

"Really?" He couldn't help but smile. "Like what?"

"Artichokes."

"Artichokes?" he parroted.

She nodded. "Steamed with lots of mayonnaise."

He made a mental note to have the chef's assistant send some artichokes to the house. Then he changed his mind and decided he should go to the market himself. He couldn't keep asking his staff to look after Julianne. She and the baby were his responsibility.

"Anything else?" Bobby asked.

"Frozen pizza."

He blinked. "You eat it frozen?"

She laughed. "No. I cook it in the microwave, so it's sort of rubbery."

"Rubbery pizza." Got it, he thought, not getting it at all. "Is that it?"

"No. I've been eating lots of chocolate, too." She

touched her tummy. "That's probably what's making me fat."

He searched for the fat, but couldn't see an ounce of anything. Maybe her T-shirt was doing a good job of hiding it.

If he could just take a peek. One little peek, so he could draw his own conclusion.

"Can I see?"

She froze. "See what? My stomach?"

"Yeah." It wasn't as if he was asking her to take off her clothes. "Just lift your shirt."

Her cheeks colored. "No."

He frowned. "Why not?"

"Because I feel stupid, showing you my binge belly."

Bobby tried not to laugh. "My kid is in there, Julianne."

"Along with forty pounds of chocolate."

"I still want to see."

"Oh, good grief." She yanked up her T-shirt, exposing her stomach.

Bobby moved closer and then grinned like a naughty schoolboy who'd just paid a girl to lift her top. Only it wasn't her breasts he was after; it was her navel.

"It's cute," he said. She did have a bit of a pooch. Just a bit.

She righted her T-shirt, then made a wide circle with her arms, clasping her hands together. "Will you think it's cute when it's out to here?"

"Yep." His baby inside her tummy made her the most beautiful woman in Texas.

She smiled, flashing her dimple, and he realized he was almost close enough to kiss her.

To taste her.

To curb his appetite.

He took a deliberate step back. Almost, he thought. But not quite.

"We should get back to work, Julianne."

"Okay." She flashed another quick, girlish smile.

He grabbed a handful of clothes, wishing he'd licked that damned dimple when he'd had the chance.

The sweet, innocent-looking dimple that made him want to get her pregnant all over again.

Nine

Julianne's first two weeks of living in Texas went by quickly. She spent a good portion of her time on the Internet, checking western apparel sites and ordering catalogs and business magazines.

On this late afternoon, she sat in front of her computer, with a glass of milk at her side, gathering information about an industry trade show hosted in Denver twice a year.

While her printer went to work, sputtering color copies, she sipped her milk and looked around. She'd transformed the den into an efficient office. It was the only room she'd redecorated, using bits and pieces of furniture she'd shipped from home.

She tried to tell herself that Texas was home now, but she hadn't quite settled in. Although she loved this cabin, with its rich, warm woods and bright colors, it still seemed like Bobby's place—a house he shouldn't have abandoned.

Every once in a while, Julianne pictured him living

here—with her. It was a crazy notion. But she couldn't help it. She wanted to erase mental images of Bobby and his wife occupying this cabin, cooking together in the kitchen, watching TV in the den, making love in the bedroom.

She had no idea what Bobby's wife had looked like, but Julianne's brain filled in the blanks, creating a flesh-and-blood woman from a ghost.

Which, she knew, wasn't a healthy thing to do. But Bobby's cautious manner when discussing his wife made her curious about the Cherokee woman he'd married.

Too curious.

She cleared her mind, and just as the printer completed its task, the doorbell pealed.

She rose to answer it and found Bobby on the other side, carrying a load of groceries.

She smiled at him. "More artichokes?"

He nodded and grinned. "Frozen pizza and candy bars, too."

"Then hurry up," she teased, anxious to delve into the chocolate. He'd been keeping her cravings in check, plying her with her favorite goodies.

After he entered the cabin, he proceeded to unload the bags, making himself at home in a kitchen that used to belong to him.

Julianne tore the wrapper on a candy bar and sank her teeth into chocolate, caramel and peanuts.

She moaned and he watched her with an amused expression.

"You have no idea how good this is." She moaned again and then realized how orgasmic she sounded.

Had she been this noisy when she and Bobby made love? Yes, she thought, looking up at him. Yes.

He reached out and smoothed a strand of her hair, and

she swallowed the food in her mouth, wishing she could taste him instead. Lick and touch and taste.

Just one more time.

"Do you want to go for a walk?" he asked, withdrawing his hand. "You've been cooped up for days."

"Okay. But I need to get my boots." And she needed to clear her head, to redirect her thoughts.

Ten minutes later she and Bobby strolled along a dirt path. The air was fresh and clean and she inhaled it generously.

He turned to look at her. "Do you want to go window-shopping on Friday? Maybe check out some baby furniture? Get some ideas for the nursery?"

She pictured them spending an afternoon in the city, gathering paint swatches and wallpaper samples. "I'd love to."

"Great." He stopped to pluck a lavender-colored flower from the grass and tuck it behind her ear. "It matches your top," he said when she merely stared.

Did he know how romantic he was? How easily he touched her heart?

She wanted to take his hand, but she wasn't sure if it would be the right thing to do. Friends didn't normally hold hands. And neither did former lovers.

"This is one of my favorite trails," he said.

"It is pretty," she agreed.

They passed a thicket of trees, where branches reached for each other and swooped overhead. Sunlight shimmered through the leaves, dappling the ground like pools of glitter.

They continued walking and she realized she'd gotten used to his limp, that she barely noticed the glitch in his stride anymore.

"Does this area seem familiar to you?" he asked.

No, but everything about him had become familiar. The

way he squinted in the sun, adjusted his hat, smiled when she least expected it.

She gathered her thoughts, tried to pay attention. "Not really. Should it?"

"We're near the main road that leads to the lodge." He guided her up a small incline, where a jackrabbit skittered by. "See?"

They stood on the side of the road and she tried to get her bearings. Pointing, she asked, "Is that the way to the lodge?"

"Nope." He turned her around. "It's this way."

As she tried to access her surroundings, a battered pickup chugged down the road, belching as it made its way toward them.

When the driver spotted them, he parked on the side of the road and climbed out of his vehicle. Tall and lanky, his face weathered from age and too much sun, he wore a dusty hat, dark jeans and a frayed shirt. He was older than his truck, considerably older, with eyes the same faded shade of blue.

"Bobby," the man said. "Glad I ran into ya." He turned, glanced at Julianne. "You showing a guest around?"

"No. This is Julianne McKenzie. She's going to manage the new boutique at the lodge. Julianne, this is Lloyd Carlton. He works at the ranch."

The older man tipped his hat and she nodded, wondering if this was how Bobby intended to introduce her to all of his employees.

Lloyd turned back to Bobby. "Where's Sharon? I ain't seen her for a while. She been commuting to the city again?"

Bobby's expression fell and suddenly he looked ill. "Sharon isn't...don't you remember, Lloyd, she..."

The old cowboy waved his hand. "It ain't no emergency. I've just got a box of pinecones for her. You tell her to swing by my trailer to collect them when she can." He tipped his hat to Julianne again. "Ma'am."

She watched him walk away, with Bobby standing beside her as haunted as an unmarked grave.

As the truck disappeared down the road, he didn't say a word. He just shoved his shaky hands into his pockets.

"What's wrong, Bobby? What just happened?"

He blinked and shifted his gaze. "Sometimes Lloyd confuses the present with the past."

The present. The past. Someone named Sharon.

Dear God, she thought, as Lloyd's confusion became clear.

"Was Sharon your wife?" she asked, even though she already knew.

"Yes." He blew out an audible breath. "Lloyd's never done that before. He's never mentioned Sharon, not once since she died."

"I'm sorry, Bobby."

"I can handle his ramblings. I can. This just…" He released another breath. "Sharon decorated pinecones during the holidays. And now Lloyd's collecting them for her, stuffing them away in a box."

Julianne waited for Bobby to say something else about Sharon, but he didn't. He clammed up, silent and grim.

"You must have loved her very much."

He frowned. "Of course I loved her. A man is supposed to love his wife. He's supposed to…"

Supposed to what? she wondered, struck by the torment in his eyes.

They stood silently for a moment and it almost seemed like a period of bereavement, a time for a quiet prayer.

"I guess it was just as well," he said suddenly. "Now

you've met Lloyd. Now you'll understand if he doesn't make any sense.''

''Does he have Alzheimer's?'' she asked, stunned by how quickly Bobby masked his emotions.

''No. He came back from the Korean War that way. In those days they called it shell shock, but no one uses that term anymore.'' Bobby removed his hands from his pockets and wiped his palms on his jeans, as if they'd turned sweaty. ''Some doctors believe he has a form of post-traumatic stress syndrome, but others say it's more of a mental illness than an anxiety disorder. Either way, Lloyd gets confused. Not all the time, though. He'll be fine for weeks, even months, then it just kicks in again.''

''How long has he worked for you?''

''Since the beginning. The bank foreclosed on his ranch about the time I built Elk Ridge. He was a neighbor of Michael's, someone the boy and his mother cared about. I had to give him a job. I had to do something.''

Because you're a good man, she thought. A kind, generous, tortured man. She wanted to take him into her arms and hold him, but she knew she couldn't.

His shoulders were rigid, the muscles tense.

''Some folks in the area were leery of Lloyd,'' he said. ''Calling him crazy and such. But Michael and his mother weren't afraid of him. His condition didn't scare them.''

''What about your guests? Does he ever frighten them?''

''He doesn't work directly with our guests, and those who do come into contact with him seem to like him. Lloyd's an authority on the Old West, and that fascinates most of our visitors.''

Julianne wondered if Lloyd would mention the pinecones again or if he would simply forget why he'd been collecting them. ''Was he close to Sharon?''

Bobby looked away. ''As close as he could be, I guess.

She only lived here for a year. He didn't know her that well.'' He shifted his stance, glanced back. "Maria looks after Lloyd. She spends a lot of time with him.''

"Maria? Your receptionist?''

"Yes. She and Lloyd are friends.''

"The way we're friends?'' Julianne asked.

"Yes.''

Lloyd and Maria had been lovers, she realized. A long time ago, before Lloyd had gone off to war, before his mind had scattered.

"Let's go,'' Bobby said. "I'll walk you back.''

As they headed down the path on which they'd come, Julianne glanced at his hand and saw the gold band shining on his finger.

Suddenly her heart ached. It hurt with a feeling she couldn't define, a feeling that jumbled her emotions.

No wonder Lloyd thought Bobby's wife was still alive. His wedding ring probably confused the old man.

As much as it confused her.

Bobby felt the need to talk, so after he walked Julianne home, he looked for Michael and found him right where he was supposed to be.

The younger man sat at his cluttered desk at the lodge, his computer screen displaying the spreadsheets he'd been working on. He spent more time in Elk Ridge's primary office than Bobby did, a workspace much bigger than the one they shared at the barn.

Michael looked up. "What's going on?

"Nothing. Just checking on you,'' he said, not quite sure what he expected to accomplish by this visit. The boy had his own problems, his own demons to contend with.

"How's your lady?'' Michael asked.

Bobby frowned. "She's not my lady.''

"Really?" Michael gave him an innocent look. "And here I thought you were the one who got her pregnant. Gee, now I'm wondering how that baby got in her belly."

"Smart ass," Bobby muttered back, even though he wanted to smile.

Michael shrugged and then grinned. "At least tell me when it happened."

"How? When? What difference does it make?"

"Was it on her birthday? You two were pretty cozy at the bar that night. Stayed later than everyone else, as I recall."

"So?"

"So I'll bet that's the night you did it. Boy, that's some birthday present you gave her."

Bobby shook his head, waiting for his nephew's self-serving grin to vanish. "I didn't come here to discuss the details with you, wise guy."

"No, I guess not." Michael turned and shut down his computer. "So why are you here? What's really going on?"

"I was with Julianne today, and then we ran into Lloyd."

"And?"

"And he said some odd things. He mentioned Sharon, spoke about her as if she were still alive."

"Oh, man. I'm sorry."

"It was strange, especially in front of Julianne."

"Are you okay?" Michael asked.

"I'm fine," he said, unable to voice his fears. What would Julianne think of him if she knew the truth? If he told her what he'd done to his wife? No one knew the dishonorable details about the accident, not even Michael.

"She's important to you," his nephew said.

"Who? Julianne? Of course she's important to me. She's having my baby."

"Funny how history repeats itself. First my dad and now you."

Bobby met Michael's gaze, knowing exactly what he meant. Cam hadn't married Celeste and Bobby wasn't going to marry Julianne.

"It's complicated," he said, studying his nephew's strong, chiseled features.

Michael looked so much like Cam, so much like Bobby's brother, with his long, loose hair and dangerous charm.

When Bobby was a kid, he'd wanted to be like Cam. To walk with a swagger, to talk fast and hard, to make tough men wary and beautiful women hungry. But that had been idol worship, a younger sibling in awe of the older one.

"Do you still wish your dad would have come through for you?" he asked. "Or doesn't it matter anymore?"

"It still matters. But you matter more. You're the one who changed my life." Michael leaned forward, his dark eyes flecked with emotion. "If it weren't for you, I'd probably be in jail. Or trying to escape the law. We both know I was headed for trouble."

"You turned yourself around. You were willing to change."

Michael shuffled some papers on his desk, but his gaze never wavered. "That's true. But at least you never gave up on me."

Because he loved Michael, even more than he'd loved Cam. Probably more than he'd ever loved anyone. "I was hard on you."

"You had to be."

And at times he still was. Bobby would always worry about Michael. The boy still had a restless side.

He looked at his nephew's desk and shook his head.

Folders, files, memos, unanswered mail, discarded junk food wrappers. The boy had a messy side, too.

"I think you should marry her, Uncle."

Bobby's heartbeat blasted his chest. He didn't need another conscience, another troubled voice. "Don't do this to me, Mike."

"But it isn't fair to the baby."

"I'll be good to my son or daughter. I'll do whatever I can to make the child's life secure. That baby means everything to me."

"I know. But it'll still be a bastard." Michael blew a rough breath, pushed his chair back and glanced at the wet bar. "I could use some coffee. Do you want some?"

Bobby tried to act casual, tried to act as if his heart wasn't steeped in guilt. "That sludge you make?"

"I suppose not." The younger man rose to pour himself a cup of the thick, dark brew. "I just wanted to tell you how I feel."

"And I respect your feelings. I understand them. Hell, I'm the one who instilled those values in you."

Michael tasted the coffee. He stood near the window, the light shining behind him. "That's right, you did. And you told me that if I ever got a girl pregnant I should marry her. That I shouldn't do what my dad did."

"This is different."

"Is it, Uncle?"

"Yes, it is," Bobby said, although at the moment he couldn't find the words to explain why.

On Friday morning the doorbell rang, sending Julianne rushing from the bathroom into the living room, fussing with her appearance along the way. She wasn't expecting Bobby, not this early. She was dressed, but she'd yet to do her hair or makeup.

Why didn't he call? Warn her that he was on his way?

Breathless, she answered the door and discovered Maria on the other side.

The Latina woman smiled. "Señorita Julianne, I came to welcome you." She held up a platter of what appeared to be brownies. "You've been here almost three weeks. I should have stopped by sooner."

Touched, Julianne accepted the gift. "They smell heavenly."

"I made them especially for you. Señor Bobby says you have cravings."

"Yes, thank you." She felt her heart flutter, her mind race. Bobby had been talking about her to his employees? "Come in, please."

She offered Maria a cup of tea and they sat at the breakfast nook, sipping chamomile and enjoying double-fudge brownies.

"Señor Bobby is happy man."

"He is?"

"*Sí*, yes. Very happy about the baby."

"I'm happy, too." She touched her tummy. "I've always wanted children. Do you have a family?"

"No. No husband, no babies." Maria laughed, patted her salt-and-pepper hair. "I'm too old now."

So am I, Julianne thought. Older than most first-time moms. She looked at Maria and wondered if the woman was still in love with Lloyd, if he was the man she'd hoped, many years before, to marry and have children with.

"Did you grow up in this area?" Julianne asked.

"*Sí*, and I've worked here since Señor Bobby built the ranch."

Then Maria had been around when Bobby had married Sharon. The mystery wife. The ghost. The lady Julianne wanted to know more about.

Dare she ask?

She reached for another brownie. One simple question wouldn't hurt. She lived in Sharon's old house. She had a right to be curious about her.

"Maria?"

"¿Sí?" The woman glanced up from her tea. She sat at the cozy table, the morning sun spilling in from the window beside her, illuminating her colorful cotton blouse.

"Did you know Bobby's wife very well?"

Maria sighed. "Sí, yes, I knew Sharon. But I did not approve of her. I felt badly about that later. So ashamed."

For a moment Julianne merely stared. Maria didn't appear to be judgmental, a person who would discount someone so readily.

"Why did you disapprove?"

"I thought she was too young for Señor Bobby."

"Too young?" A familiar pain shocked Julianne's system. A pain of betrayal. A pain of disbelief. "How old was she?"

"Twenty when they started dating, twenty-one when they married. Sharon was the same age as Señor Michael, not Señor Bobby. To me, it seemed strange. Mixed up, no?"

"Yes." Strange. Mixed up. Hurtful. Bobby's wife had been as young as his nephew, as young as the boy he'd raised—seventeen years his junior.

Yet Bobby had never said a word, not one single word. Not even when Julianne had confided in him about her ex-husband's affair with a younger woman.

"Was Sharon pretty?" she asked, fighting tears.

"Sí. Very pretty. A college student." Maria dropped her gaze. "I should not have disapproved of her."

Julianne blinked back another threat of tears, doing her

damnedest to steel her emotions, to tell herself that Bobby's past didn't matter.

She wouldn't cry, damn it. She wouldn't lose her composure over this.

Maria looked up. "I never told Señor Bobby how I felt. I did not think it was my place."

Is it my place? Julianne wondered, battling the ache in her chest. *My right to confront him?*

Or should she let it go? Ignore it? Pretend she'd never found out?

"Maybe we should talk about something else," Maria suggested. "Something happier."

Julianne nodded and then faked her way through a lighthearted conversation.

Fifteen minutes later, after Maria left, she went back into the bathroom to finish getting ready.

To work on her appearance, to look presentable, to stay strong.

But even after she'd curled her hair and applied cosmetics to her face, she knew her efforts were in vain.

She'd made herself look as pretty as possible, but no matter how hard she tried, she couldn't make herself twenty again.

She couldn't compete with Bobby's attraction to younger women.

And because she couldn't, she turned away from the mirror and started to cry.

In the next instant her knees buckled and she sank to the floor, allowing tears to flood the gaping hole in her heart.

Ten

Bobby left the barn and climbed into his truck, preparing to get Julianne for their outing.

What was he going to do about her? About the frustration? The need? The all-consuming attraction?

He couldn't marry her, he couldn't bring her that deeply into his life. Yet he wanted to make love with her.

He took the tree-flanked path, barely conscious of the road, of the climbing and descending hills, of the picture-perfect scenery leading the way.

If he didn't get this off his chest, he was going to explode. Which meant he had to talk to Julianne.

And say what? "I want you to be my lover?"

Why did this have to be so damned complicated? Why couldn't he just remain friends with her?

Because he wanted her too badly, that's why.

And he suspected she wanted him, too.

Bobby arrived at her doorstep in a bundle of masculine

nerves, preparing his speech and faltering with every anticipated word.

There would be terms attached to a sexual relationship,
conditions Julianne would have to accept. And he wasn't
sure how to broach the subject.

Finally he gave up and rang the bell. He didn't have to
rush into this. He could play it by ear, say it when the
moment seemed right.

She didn't answer, so he pressed the button again. Where
was she? He knew she had been looking forward to their
outing, to getting ideas on decorating the nursery.

A minute later he checked his watch. It wasn't like Julianne to be late.

Once again he tried the bell, but this time when she
didn't answer, he panicked. What if something had happened to her? To the baby?

Because he didn't have a key to the cabin on him, he
reached into his pocket for his cell phone, but he came up
empty.

He'd left his cell at the barn.

Damn it.

Not knowing what else to do, he tried the door, praying
it was unlocked.

When it opened he thanked the Creator and rushed inside, calling her name.

"Julianne!"

She didn't respond.

He tried the master bedroom first, afraid of what he
might find. But the room was empty, the bed neatly made.

Then he heard muffled sobs coming from the adjoining
bathroom. Without thinking, he pushed open the door.

She sat on the tiled floor, her knees drawn to her chest,
crying like a shattered little fairy.

Dear God.

"Julianne." He said her name softly and she looked up. "What's wrong, honey? What happened?" He crouched on the floor in front of her. "Are you hurt? Is it the baby?"

"No." She wiped her tears and got to her feet.

He rose to his full height, as well. "Did you get bad news from home?"

"No." She gulped a shaky-sounding breath and grabbed a box of tissues from the counter. "I just felt like crying."

He watched her dry her face. "Why? Tell me why."

She gazed at him with dark-rimmed eyes. Sad, lonely eyes. "It doesn't matter."

"Yes it does. It has something to do with me, doesn't it?" He could feel the painful connection, the emotion that bound them. "I did something to hurt you."

"I don't have any right to feel this way." She blew her nose and tossed the tissues into the trash. "But I can't help it."

"Feel what way?"

Her breath hitched. "Betrayed."

His heart went still. "I betrayed you? How?"

"You didn't tell me how young Sharon was. Why didn't you tell me, Bobby?"

Oh, God. He looked into her eyes and saw his own shame. "I'm sorry. It isn't easy for me to talk about my wife. To go into all that."

"I know. But it makes me feel so old." She started crying again. "So ugly."

"No." He shook his head and reached for her, pulling her into his arms. She buried her face against his chest and continued to cry. "You're not old and you're not ugly. You're in the prime of your life and you're beautiful." He pressed his lips to the top of her head. "So beautiful."

She pulled back to look up at him and he could see that she didn't believe him.

"I thought you were beautiful from the first moment I saw you," he told her, hoping she would see herself through his eyes. "You bewitched me. You still do." He slid his hand to her tummy. "And you're having my baby. No other woman has given me a child."

"But your wife was only twenty-one when you married her, Bobby. That's so young."

"It wasn't her age that first attracted me to her. It was the similarity in our backgrounds, our culture." He paused, explaining the best he could. "We were both raised in traditional homes, with some of the same ideals. The same spiritual beliefs."

She sniffed and dried her eyes. "Her age was never a factor?"

He shrugged and tried to contain the tightness in his chest, the guilt that surrounded Sharon's memory. "I was flattered that she was interested in me. It was exciting in the beginning. But the newness wore off."

"I don't believe you. How can being around a young, beautiful woman wear off? How can that kind of excitement ever go away?"

"I don't know. It just did." He wasn't sure what to say, how to delve into this without revealing too much. Sharon was dead. He'd put her in the grave. How could he speak ill of her? He glanced at his ring, faced the clench of the past. "Sometimes she argued about things I thought were silly. And sometimes she wanted more attention than I could give her."

"Why?"

He tried for a little humor, hoping it would dull the ache. "Maybe I was just old and boring. Turning gray too fast."

"I should have tried it," she said. "I should have found a young lover."

Bobby frowned. "Why? Because guys with gray hair are losing their appeal?"

She made a teasing face. "Maybe."

"Oh, yeah?" He tickled the side of her rib cage and they both laughed.

A second later they fell silent, two people caught in an emotional situation.

"I need to fix my makeup," she said. "I'll be ready in a few minutes."

Bobby wondered how long she'd been crying, how long she'd been curled up on the cold floor sobbing over him.

"Are you sure you're up for this, Julianne? We can go into the city tomorrow."

She gave him a brave smile. "I'm fine. And I want to go today."

"Okay." He watched her turn away to repair her smudged mascara.

She looked so delicate, he thought, in her silky blouse and floral-printed skirt. Her eyes were slightly swollen, her nose chafed, her hair mussed.

The bathroom counter held a collection of creams, lotions, sprays and gels. He reached for her perfume and fingered the bottle, tracing the curvaceous shape of the glass.

Julianne caught his gaze in the mirror and suddenly he longed to kiss her, to taste her, to lose himself in the warmth of her skin, the fresh-meadow scent of her hair.

Bobby replaced the perfume and took a steadying breath.

He might as well get that gut-churning speech out of the way. Waiting wouldn't do either of them any good.

"Julianne?"

She added a dab of powder to her nose, then turned around. "Yes?"

"There's something I think we should discuss."

She tilted her head, waiting for him to continue, and he

worried if he'd spoken too soon, if he was truly ready to confront this conversation.

But backing out now would be cowardly and he didn't fancy himself with a yellow streak down his belly.

"This is about sex," he said.

Her mouth formed a silent "Oh," and he realized how blunt he'd sounded.

Good going, he thought. Real smooth. Real romantic.

Romantic? Bobby frowned, jammed his hands into his pockets. Since when were disabled men considered idyllic lovers?

"I want to be with you again," he told her, wishing his palms hadn't begun to sweat. "Are you still interested in me?"

She nodded and he wondered if her heart was pounding as rapidly as his.

"It's impossible for me to treat this casually," he said. "To just take off my clothes and jump into bed. If we make love again, it will be like before. Do you understand what I'm saying?"

"I think so." With restless fingers, she picked up her compact and fiddled with it, opening the case, then snapping it shut. "I'll be naked, and you'll be half dressed."

Feeling awkward, he shrugged. "It's easier for me that way."

But explaining why was impossible. Imagining himself as a whole man when he was with Julianne was the only way he could cope with the intimacy that came with sex.

He couldn't bear for her to look at his residual limb, to touch it, to ponder the accident that was a blatant reminder of why he was an amputee.

"I saw a picture of a runner with a prosthetic leg. It was metal." She paused, toyed with her compact again. "What kind do you have?"

Damn it, he thought.

Technical curiosity. He should have expected it, been prepared for it. "I have several. And they're designed to look like my other leg. The components are padded and covered with a protective skin." He tried to sound casual, to let her think this wasn't bothering him as badly as it was. "The feet attached to my prostheses are called a cowboy high heel, designed for the shape of a boot."

She moved a little closer. "So you can wear any boot you want?"

"My boots are custom made, with a zipper."

He saw her trying to calculate why, trying to picture the angle of an inanimate leg, a fake foot.

"Do you ever wear your prosthesis to bed?"

Did she assume that he concealed it under a pair of pajamas? The way he did with his jeans? "No one does. Or they shouldn't, anyway."

"You'll never spend the night with me? Never sleep beside me?"

"No." He knew some women liked to cuddle after sex, to keep their partners close throughout the night, but that wasn't in the cards. "If you can't handle this, that's fine. I just wanted to get it out in the open."

She met his gaze. "I can handle it."

"So you're willing to be my lover?"

"If you're sure you're willing to do it with a forty-year-old crybaby."

He couldn't stop the smile that ghosted across his lips. "I'm sure."

She smiled, as well. "Me, too."

He removed his hands from his pockets and wiped his clammy palms. Okay, then, it was settled. They were official lovers. Or they would be, once he initiated their next encounter.

"You better finish getting ready," he said.

She turned back to the mirror, her voice a little shy. "I'm nearly done."

"Good. Great." He stood behind her, so both of their reflections were visible. "You're not a crybaby, Julianne. You're perfect," he added softly.

Simply perfect.

Baby Bonus, a retail store stocked with furniture, clothing, bedding, strollers, high chairs, car seats and toys, offered the best selection in town.

Julianne and Bobby wandered the aisles, checking out every display.

"I like this," he said, stopping to admire a white crib trimmed in red. "The bedding is nice, too."

Julianne studied the sunburst print on the quilt. The man who lived in darkness and seclusion seemed determined to decorate the nursery in bright, vivid colors.

"I like it, too." She could imagine their baby sleeping in a room bursting with sunshine and candied apples. She moved toward a tiny rocking chair and smiled at the teddy bear occupying it. "He's cute."

Bobby came up behind her, slipping his arms around her waist. "This setup would work for a boy or a girl."

Julianne leaned back, relaxing against his body. He felt so strong, so right. A big, brawny cowboy who would protect his family, keep them safe and warm.

Am I part of his family? she wondered. Did conceiving his child make her more than a friend? More than a lover?

She kept telling herself that his refusal to undress in front of her wasn't a big deal. Yet deep down she knew it was.

Maybe the problem was more than just shedding his clothes. Maybe Bobby wasn't capable of giving a woman the security she needed.

He'd admitted that his wife had wanted more from him, that she'd argued over what he considered silly things.

Yet he still wore his wedding ring. A gold band that seemed far too significant.

So don't think about that, Julianne told herself. Don't dwell on Bobby's past. Think about the future, about the child they'd created.

She placed her hand over his, cradling their baby.

Wasn't a child more significant than a ring?

As he nibbled her ear, a delicious stream of pleasure snaked up her spine.

"I can't wait to touch you," he whispered.

He was touching her now, but she knew he spoke of something much more intimate.

"When will it happen?" she asked almost as quietly.

He slid his hands from her waist to her breasts, rubbing his thumbs over her nipples. "When do you want it to happen?"

Instantly aroused, Julianne pressed her bottom against his fly. "Tonight."

A hardness pressed back and she let a wave of dizziness wash over her.

Voices sounded at the end of the aisle. Bobby dropped his hands and she righted her posture and shot her gaze in the direction of the noise. Other shoppers. Another pregnant couple.

"Sorry," Bobby said.

"That's okay. I don't think they saw us."

He cleared his throat. "Hope not."

An unexpected smile twitched her lips. He always cleared his throat when he was nervous. Or embarrassed. Or battling to banish naughty thoughts.

Intrigued, she debated on hugging him, on holding on

and never letting go. Suddenly she felt young again. Young and in love.

In love?

"We should buy him."

"What?" She blinked, tried to calm her jumping pulse.

"The teddy bear." Bobby strode over to the rocking chair and picked up the stuffed animal. "It'll be the baby's first toy."

A blast of panic struck her hard and quick. She'd fallen in love with him. This wasn't supposed to happen. She wasn't supposed to let her emotions go that far.

He wiggled the bear's arms, making it dance, and she took a much-needed breath, fighting for oxygen.

"Sometimes I still can't believe this is happening." Furry brown feet kicked this time. "I'm actually going to be a dad."

She released the air in her lungs, and he smiled.

"Do know you what's going on in there?" The teddy bear poked a playful paw at her tummy. "The baby's not much bigger than an inch, but its facial features are already formed. It's amazing, isn't it? Our kid probably looks like us, even now."

Us. The two of them.

Of course she loved him, she thought, watching those dark eyes crinkle. How could she not?

"We should wait until the baby is born to come up with names," he said. "That's the Cherokee way."

Still struggling for composure, she merely nodded.

"In the early days, a Cherokee baby was named in a ceremony by an elder in the community. A Beloved Woman," he explained. "An older lady who held a place of honor among the people. But the name she chose wasn't always permanent. Later in life, a new name might be earned or given."

He tucked the teddy bear under his arm, clearly set on buying on it. "But things have changed. Today the father names a child."

And that was important to him, she realized. To adhere to tradition, to play a significant role in naming their baby.

"A lot of things have changed," he went on to say. "In an ancient Cherokee household, a man moved in with the woman he married, and he was restricted in his authority over the children. Now, a man is the undisputed head of the household."

She didn't know how to respond, not when his words barely applied. How could he be the head of the household when they didn't even live together?

"I want the baby to have my last name," he said.

Then marry me, Julianne thought hopelessly. Marry me.

When she remained quiet, a frown creased his brow. "Celeste did that for Michael. She gave him Cam's last name."

Because Celeste had loved your brother, she wanted to say. The way I love you.

"Is this conversation upsetting you?" he asked. "I'm not trying to discount your roots. We'll teach the baby about your heritage. About magic, myths and Irish folklore."

"I'm not upset." She looked into his eyes and saw her future, a need she couldn't deny. "Everything just seems to be happening so fast."

"I know. But we're figuring things out." He leaned into her, pulling her against his heart.

Julianne closed her eyes and listened to the strong, steady beats, praying that somewhere deep inside of him, he'd begun to fall in love with her, too.

Eleven

Hours after the shopping spree, Bobby pulled his truck onto the ranch and then remembered that he'd left his cell phone at the barn.

Should he stop now? Or deal with it later?

Now, he decided. He needed a few minutes to gather his wits, to prepare for the lovemaking ahead.

He didn't know if he should bring Julianne to his house or to hers. If he should burn candles, play soft music or draw a herbal-scented bath and let her relax first, soak in the tub by herself.

He wanted to do right by Julianne. But these days, romance eluded him.

When he looked over at her, she smiled, as spellbinding as an enchanted sprite. Orchids bloomed on her skirt and fire danced in her hair, warming his blood.

Bobby could almost taste the heat, the flames licking his skin. And like the hungry male he was, he could imagine taking her here, in the truck, with stars peeking down from a darkening sky.

In his truck? Was he crazy?

He hadn't had sex in a vehicle since he'd lost his virginity. And even then, he'd been nervous, an anxious teenage boy lacking finesse.

Apparently romance had eluded him in those days, too.

"I have to swing by my office," he said, parking at the side of the barn. "I left my cell phone there. Do you want to come in or would you prefer to wait here?"

"I'll go with you."

She brushed his hand and he steadied his breath. He couldn't remember wanting a woman as badly as he wanted Julianne. Not even Sharon.

Don't go there, he told himself guiltily. Don't compare your new lover to your dead wife.

They exited the truck and walked the short path to the building. Security lamps burned softly and a mild breeze blew, scenting the air with night-blooming fragrances.

He guided Julianne into the barn and they went straight to his office. He flipped on a light and closed the door, automatically locking it behind him.

"I'll only be a minute. Of course, I should probably check my messages."

"Take your time. Is it okay if I make a cup of tea?"

"I don't think I've got any tea. But I'm pretty sure there's some hot chocolate. The instant stuff with the little marshmallows."

"That sounds even better."

She headed for the kitchenette and he sat at his desk and found his phone. So what was he going to do? Whose house should he take her to?

He supposed hers would be the logical choice. His might

seem too presumptuous, even if she had agreed to be with him tonight.

By the time Bobby checked his messages, Julianne stood behind him, sipping chocolate.

She leaned over and put the cup on his desk. "I've been dying to unbraid your hair. To see how long it is."

He didn't turn around. "Really?"

"Mmm. Would you mind, Bobby?"

He closed his eyes. She was asking for permission to touch him, to send erotic shivers up and down his spine. "No, I don't mind."

She unbound the braid gently, working her hands into his hair, combing through the dark mass with agile fingers.

"It's beautiful," she said.

He opened his eyes, felt his body harden. "So is yours. I have fantasies about your hair, Julianne." He turned in his chair, then rose to kiss her.

Their lips met, as warm and moist as a summer rain. She tasted sweet, like swirling chocolate and melting marshmallows. He stroked her tongue; she sucked on his. Within seconds, they were devouring each other in a hot, voracious kiss.

He pulled back and their gazes locked and held. "I've been going crazy. Wondering how to please you. What to do to make this right."

"Just love me," she said.

"Here? Now?"

"Yes."

That was all it took. One word. One need.

He reached for her blouse and unbuttoned it. The silk melted in his hands as he let it fall to the floor. Her skirt came next. He slid the pleated circle down her hips and she stepped out of the elastic waistband.

Bobby couldn't have dreamed this; he couldn't have planned for it to unfold the way it did.

She stood in front of him in a white bra and simple panties. She looked so delicate, so trusting, in bits of cotton and lace.

He took a moment to appreciate that her legs were bare, that she wore nothing but skin.

Smooth, creamy skin.

When he unhooked her bra and discarded it, he filled his hands with her breasts.

Soft, he thought as he rubbed his thumbs around the darkened areolas. "Pretty," he said out loud as her nipples hardened from his touch.

Anxious, he went after her panties, and she held on to his shoulders while he removed them.

He guided her toward the chair. She sat and looked up at him, clearly wondering what he had in store.

Bobby lowered himself to the floor, finding a comfortable position in front of her. Recognition dawned in her eyes and he smiled.

She still wore her shoes, a pair of strappy sandals that tied around her ankles. He tugged at the crisscross of leather.

"Bondage," he said.

She laughed, her hair falling forward, draping her face. "I'm a little kinky."

"So am I." He grabbed her hips, scooted her to the edge of the chair and pulled her toward his mouth.

The air in her lungs whooshed out and he knew he'd aroused her good and proper.

She bucked on contact and he took what he wanted, what they both craved. He tasted her, encouraging her to press closer, to rub against him.

He deepened his next kiss, licking and teasing, swirling

with his tongue. She arched her back and made a needy sound.

Nothing mattered but this moment, he thought.

This feeling. This woman.

She played with his unbound hair, touched his face, his mouth, his tongue. He licked her fingers and pressed them inside of her, making her stroke herself.

She gasped and he glanced up her. She looked down at him and, for a moment, they just stared at each other.

It was, he thought, the single most erotic instant of his life.

He kissed her again, as intimately as he could.

Julianne climaxed against his mouth, her body going taunt, then molten, then taut again.

Bobby rose to his feet, taking her with him.

Desire churned, stiff and erect in his jeans. He could still taste her release, the sweet, musky flavor.

He lifted her onto his desk, tore off his shirt and battled his belt.

His breath burned his throat; his mind went foggy. He fought for control, told himself to slow down.

Don't hurry. Don't let this end too soon.

He unzipped his pants, waited a beat, freed himself.

When he slipped into her, Julianne pulled her hands through his hair.

He quivered like a stallion, nibbling her neck, breathing in her scent. She wrapped her legs around him, and he bit back the urge to take, to ravish.

With care, with caution, he moved, determined to love her reverently.

She kissed him in response and he slid his hands over her breasts, around her hips and let the sensation linger on her tummy.

She touched him, too, caressing muscle and bone, hard edges and rough planes.

He pushed deeper, increased the rhythm, pleasuring himself, arousing her.

They danced on water, on a wave as mystical as the shimmer in her eyes, as green as a Celtic sea. Time passed and his heart beat with every stroke, every rocking motion.

Sighs, sweet surrender, unspoken promises.

When she climaxed, he could have sworn he'd seen it happen, seen it swirl through her body in a prism of melting colors.

In the glowing aftermath she blinked and smiled, bringing him closer.

Unable to refuse the invitation, Bobby spilled into her and let himself fall, collapsing in the warm, willing circle of his lover's arms.

The following day Bobby did his damnedest to stay away. He worked with the horses, tried to keep his mind busy, his body labored.

But both kept thinking about Julianne.

Cursing his weakness, he got in his truck, hoped he'd find her at home. He drove too fast, slowed down, considered turning back to the barn.

But in the end, he kept heading in her direction, too damn anxious to be near her, to ask her on a date.

Not a good sign, he told himself.

But hey, he was only human. And the sex had been incredible. Why wouldn't he want to spend more time with her?

He parked in front of the cabin and saw her sitting on the porch steps, with Chester at her side.

What was that mutt doing here? The big lummox had his head in her lap, probably drooling all over her dress.

Bobby got out of his truck, and Julianne acknowledged him, but the first words out of her mouth were about the dog.

"He just showed up at my doorstep," she said, scratching behind Chester's Dumbo ears. "Do you think he's a stray?"

Bobby gave Chester a narrow-eyed look and the mutt snuggled closer to Julianne. "That's Michael's dog. The most spoiled beast you'd ever want to meet."

"Really? He doesn't act spoiled."

Was she kidding? "He eats table scraps, whines for attention and sleeps on Michael's bed. Believe me, Chester gets whatever he wants."

"Chester? Oh, that's cute." She kissed the top of the mutt's ugly head. "You're a good boy, aren't you?"

Yeah, a good boy. Bobby sat next to the dog and Chester snubbed his nose at him.

"What are you trying to pull?" he asked the dog, nudging the mixed breed with his elbow.

Chester made a pathetic sound.

"Oh, I get it. Your redhead wasn't available today, so you're moving in on mine."

"Are you referring to me?" Julianne asked, her eyes bright and curious.

Too curious.

Uncomfortable, Bobby shrugged. Why did women have to analyze everything a man said? "That was guy talk."

"Guy talk?"

"Chester has a crush on an Irish setter."

"A redhead," she commented.

"Yeah, and I told him about you and me. That we had sex and made a baby."

"You told the dog…oh, my." She turned away, restraining a giggle.

"It seemed like the thing to do at the time." He frowned at the back of her head. "Knock it off, Julianne. It isn't funny."

"Yes, it is."

When she turned back around, Chester woofed and she gave in and laughed. Her dimple surfaced, then disappeared, playing an intriguing game of peekaboo.

Bobby smiled, taking a moment to enjoy the woman and the dog.

A few quiet minutes later she asked, "Do you want some iced tea?"

"Sure." He followed her inside, Chester on their heels.

She'd spruced up the house with potted plants and baskets of dried flower petals, adding touches of who she was.

Spending time at his old place wasn't as difficult as he'd assumed it would be. At least not with Julianne here, making the cabin seem like a home again.

She handed him a tall glass of tea sweetened with sugar and garnished with a lemon wedge.

"Thanks." He took a sip, deciding Julianne looked like a wood nymph with her garden-printed dress and bare feet.

No wonder Chester couldn't resist her. The dog sat on the tiled floor, staring up at her with big, droopy eyes.

"Is it all right if I feed him?" she asked.

"I don't see why not. Michael gives him all kinds of junk."

She opened the fridge and came up with some leftover corned beef and cabbage. Chester wiggled as she picked through it, separating a few slices of beef and placing them in a plastic bowl.

The dog gulped up what she gave him. Chester should probably get used to Irish meals, Bobby thought, considering he had his heart set on an Irish setter.

"Do you think I could try some of that?" he asked.

"Oh, of course." She spooned the rest of the leftovers onto a plate and heated it in the microwave.

When it was ready, she handed it to him, along with a fork and a bottle of vinegar.

He eyed the bottle warily. "What am I supposed to do with this?"

"Season your meal. Haven't you ever eaten corned beef and cabbage before?"

"No." But he was determined to acquire a taste for it, the way he'd acquired a taste for petite redheads.

She watched him take a bite and he tried not to feel self-conscious. He'd awakened this morning wishing she were beside him and cursing the reason she wasn't.

"Well?" she asked.

"It's good." The vinegar gave the cabbage and potatoes a tangy flavor. "Different. I like it."

"It's easy to make."

"Then you can teach me sometime."

"Okay."

When their conversation faltered, he continued eating, wondering why he was nervous today. He shouldn't be, not after last night. Of course, there was the matter of that date.

"There's a barn dance coming up," he ventured to say.

"Really?"

"It'll be similar to the one we had when your cousins were here. We have them fairly often."

"When is it?"

"Tuesday. The chef is planning an Italian menu. He used to do a country barbecue every time, but these days he likes the idea of creating an international theme. He hasn't done an Irish one yet, though. He's probably waiting for Saint Patrick's Day." Bobby rinsed his plate and placed it in the dishwasher, trying to keep his cool. Suddenly he felt like a tall, gawky kid preparing to ask the prettiest girl in school to the prom. "Do you want to go with me?"

She smiled, brushed her feathery bangs out of her eyes. "That sounds nice. Fun."

Because Bobby couldn't think of anything else to say, he made a show of checking his watch, wishing he could cart her off to the bedroom instead. "Well, I guess I better go. I've still got a few more lessons this afternoon." He paused, glanced at the mutt. "I can take Chester back to Michael's."

"That's okay. He can stay."

Chester panted and Bobby rolled his eyes.

Julianne laughed. "You two are funny together."

"You think him trying to steal my girl is funny?" Bobby swept her into his arms and gave her the kiss he'd been craving all day, a sexy assault of mouth, tongue and teeth.

She staggered afterward.

"Are you sure you have to go?"

His pulse shot up his arm. "Maybe I can stay."

"Maybe?" she challenged.

"Definitely." He didn't care if he was late for his next appointment, if he dropped everything to be with her, to have her. "I can stay." He grabbed her, kissed her again. "But we'll have to make this fast." And hot and hard, he thought. The excitement they both craved.

He looked around the kitchen and backed her into the herb closet, the room he'd designed for drying medicinal plants. The counters were scattered with wildflowers she'd collected and the heady scent rose to his nostrils.

It was perfect. It spoke of her. Of the woman who cherished the sun, the moon, the vibrant blooms that dotted the hills. Julianne, with her garden-printed dress and wind-tousled hair.

He lifted her onto the floral-laden counter and she tipped her head back. So warm, so willing, so fragrant.

With as much finesse as he could muster, he opened the front of her dress and fought a vicious war to not rip the damn thing off, to send buttons popping.

She leaned forward to kiss him and he battled the hooks on her bra.

As he sucked in a barely controlled breath, her breasts filled his hands and her dress bunched around her hips, leaving her panties to his disposal.

He yanked them off and she went after him.

She snagged his belt, flipped open the buckle and deliberately brushed his fly.

She looked wildly erotic half dressed, tugging at his shirt and unzipping his jeans.

What was left of their clothes didn't matter. They would make love around them. Fast, furious—the way they both wanted it.

She stroked him, making him more aroused than he could endure. Feral, anxious, he thrust into her, plunging deep.

With a gasp, she wrapped her legs around him, locking him in, taking him deeper. His lady, his lover, the wood nymph with her beguiling dimples and bare feet.

Warm and wet, she moved with him. The tempo set his mind spinning, his vision blurring.

She arched against him, wanting more.

So he gave, all that he was capable of. Every brand stemmed from his blood, every hot, demanding thrill from the edge of his sanity.

She dug her nails into his shoulder, and he thrust harder. He took her, with greed, with passion, with masculine fury.

And when she climaxed, when she cried out his name, he dragged her tight against him and emptied his body desperately into hers.

On Tuesday evening, Julianne got ready early, preparing for the night ahead. She hadn't seen much of Bobby since he'd asked her to the dance, but they'd both been busy.

Ranch activities took up most of his time and preparations for the boutique had been keeping her occupied.

She'd ordered some samples, including a hand-embroidered shirt from an up-and-coming designer. A shirt she'd purchased in Bobby's size. Or so she hoped. She wasn't certain about his measurements.

She went to the bedroom and took the shirt out of the box. It had arrived this morning and she intended to give it to him tonight, hoping he would wear it to the dance.

She rewrapped the garment, insisting she owed Bobby a visit. How many times had he stopped by her cabin, bearing gifts?

He'd never brought her clothes, but he supplied her with plenty of chocolate.

With her confidence bolstered, she tucked the package under her arm and got in her car. Taking the bumpy road to his house, she listened to the radio.

Within the hour she would be dancing in Bobby's arms. And within a few minutes she would be standing on his porch.

The man she loved.

When she rapped on his door, her heart pounded with every knock. Foolish girl, she thought suddenly. She should have stayed home and waited for him to pick her up.

But no, she'd found an excuse to foist herself on him.

He opened the door just then and she knew—oh, God, she knew—she had truly made a mistake.

He didn't speak. Not a word. He flinched, frowned, flinched again.

Balancing himself on crutches, he wore nothing but a pair of sweats. One leg filled the fabric, but the other dangled loosely at the bottom, where the hem had been cut.

"I thought you were Michael," he said finally. "No one comes to my house unannounced except my nephew."

"I'm sorry." Was that a privacy rule? Something everyone at the ranch automatically followed?

She ran her tongue across her teeth, felt her mouth go dry. Bobby's hair was loose, damp from a recent shower and trailing water down his bare shoulders.

"I was supposed to pick you up, Julianne."

"I know." She tried to summon a smile. His amputated leg wasn't visible, but the knowledge of it ghosted between them, making her wonder about the car accident, the surgery, the pain and depression he'd suffered. "I only stopped by to bring you something."

She handed over the box. "It's a shirt. I thought maybe you'd want to wear it tonight. If it fits, of course. It's from a new designer. I'm considering carrying her line in the boutique."

He took the package, but he held fast to his frown, to the discomfort in his eyes. "Thank you."

"You're welcome." She wished she could make this easier. But knowing she couldn't, she stepped back. How could she tell him that answering the door without his prosthesis didn't diminish his appeal? That he was a man—a strong, virile man—no matter what?

"I'll pick you up around eight," he said, letting her know, quite politely, that he had no intention of inviting her into his home. Not now. Not while he was crutching around the place.

"Maybe I'll go to the dance a little early. By myself for

a while," she added, too shaken to return to her house to wait for him. "Is that okay with you?"

"That's fine. I'll meet you there."

She said goodbye and Bobby thanked her again for the gift he'd yet to open.

An hour later Julianne sat with some guests from the ranch, feeding her nerves with Sicilian entrées from the buffet: sweet and sour eggplant, meatballs, a zucchini salad.

The international/country theme worked. The Italian food complemented the Texas barn, especially when the band played a movie score, a catchy song from one of those delightful old Spaghetti Westerns.

Just as Julianne set about to taste the watermelon pudding, Bobby arrived. He'd paired the shirt she'd given him with black jeans, a trophy-buckle belt and snakeskin boots.

He acknowledged his guests and took the chair she'd saved for him.

"I like the shirt," he said quickly. "It reminds me of rodeo garb from the fifties. I've always been into that vintage style."

Pleased that he approved, she brushed his hand, a little apprehensive to touch him. "Then I'll make sure to order them for the boutique."

He smiled and she knew he was pretending the awkward encounter at his door had never happened. Her cue, she realized, to never bring it up. To stay away from his house. Unless, of course, she'd been invited.

Suddenly she wanted to cry. For him, for her, for the wall he was building, the barrier that kept them from getting too close.

"Do you like the pudding?" he asked.

She gazed at the parfait glass in front of her. "I haven't tried it yet."

He scooted his chair closer to the table. "It's one of my favorite desserts."

"I thought you steered clear of sweets."

"I do. Usually. But I might indulge tonight. *Gelo di melone.* Even the name makes me hungry."

Without thinking, she dipped into the pudding and offered him a spoonful. He took it without hesitation and she wondered if his wife had fed him cake on their wedding day.

Once again she wanted to cry, to mourn the marriage she feared she would never have with Bobby.

He licked whipped cream from his lips. "Try some yourself."

She ate from the same spoon. "It's wonderful." And to her, it tasted of him. Of Texas nights and wishful dreams.

Together, they finished her dessert and he leaned in and brushed her cheek with a gentle kiss. "Do you want to dance?"

"I'd love to."

The music was softer now, a slow country ballad. He took her in his arms and she realized he wasn't hiding their romance.

But why would he? Everyone at the ranch knew about the baby. Everyone, she supposed, except Lloyd, who probably couldn't recall being told.

She caught sight of the old cowboy standing in a corner, watching her and Bobby with a scowl on his face.

Maria walked over to Lloyd and took his hand, guiding him outside. Julianne closed her eyes and fought the fear creeping back into her soul.

The urge to weep once again.

Twelve

Julianne stood at a fence rail, trying to shake the melancholy from the night before. After the dance Bobby had dropped her off at the cabin, given her a passionate kiss and told her he'd see her sometime today.

It had been a perfectly confusing date, with a confusing man.

And after the way he'd behaved, the way he'd twisted her emotions, she had a right to be upset.

Bobby simply wasn't letting her into his heart.

With a sigh, she gazed at the horses in pasture. A pretty palomino nibbled playfully on the coat of a gray, and a chestnut appeared to be handing down a pecking order, letting the herd know he was in charge.

"Ma'am," a voice said from behind her.

She turned to find Lloyd studying her the way she'd been studying the horses, analyzing her with watery blue eyes.

"I saw you at the dance," he said.

"I saw you, too. You were with Maria."

Lloyd squinted. His face was tanned and weathered, as hard as sunbaked leather. "Are you really having Bobby's baby?"

She gulped the air in her throat. "Yes."

"Maria claimed you was, but I didn't believe her. We argued about it."

"I'm sorry," was all Julianne could think to say.

He shifted his stance, bending one bony knee. "Maria keeps telling me that I forget things, mix up my years and such. Maybe I'm gettin' senile."

"We're all forgetful now and then," she said, hoping to comfort him. Apparently he didn't understand the magnitude of his disorder.

"Maria says Bobby's wife is dead. Is that true?"

Julianne nodded. "Sharon died three years ago."

"I don't recall her dying. I just don't." He frowned, changed his posture again, bending the other knee. "I remember when her and Bobby got married. I was at the weddin'."

"You were?"

"Yes, ma'am. They had themselves a traditional Cherokee ceremony." He made a pained face. "I can't believe that little gal is gone."

She closed her eyes, opened them a few seconds later. "I didn't know her."

"No, I suppose you didn't." Lloyd sighed. "Are you and Bobby married now?"

Her heart bumped her chest. "No."

"Then how come Bobby wears a weddin' band?"

Her legs went weak; her eyes began to water. Somehow she'd known Bobby's ring was the reason Lloyd had been keeping Sharon alive.

Was that Bobby's way of keeping her alive, too?

She inhaled a breath, willed her tears not to fall. "I guess he can't bear to remove it."

"Yet he's having a baby with you?"

"Yes."

"I don't like to stick my nose in other people's business. But Bobby should know better. He ought to marry the woman carrying his child. He ain't like his dead brother. He ain't a hellion."

No, he was a proper, responsible man, Julianne thought. But that didn't automatically bind him to her.

Would he remove his ring if she asked him to? Discuss his dead wife? The accident that had left him widowed?

She blinked, felt the sting of unshed tears. Would he undress in front of her? Trust her enough to be his partner in every way?

"I'll talk to Bobby," she told Lloyd, knowing she didn't have a choice. She couldn't go on day after day, month after month, hoping the man she loved would bare his soul.

The old cowboy stepped forward. "I'm sorry if I made you sad."

"I was sad already," she admitted. Living in denial, pretending everything was all right one moment and battling her emotions the next.

"Bobby took a group into the hills, but he should be back soon. Why don't you wait for him in his office? Get yourself a glass of milk."

"Thank you. Maybe I will."

He gave her a paternal nod and they parted company. But as she started toward the barn, he stopped her.

"Ma'am?"

She turned. "Yes?"

"What should I do with all those pinecones?"

She looked at him, saw the distress in his eyes. He was

rational today, but tomorrow he might slip into a state of confusion. "I don't know."

"Can I bring them to your place?"

God help her. She couldn't take over for Sharon, not like that. She wanted to be Bobby's future, not a replica from his past. "Why don't you scatter them in the hills? As a memorial for Sharon."

"All right." He smiled a little, content with the idea. "Now go on and get yer milk."

Once again, Julianne started toward the barn. A cool breeze blew her hair across her face. Summer had ended and fall was in the air. Soon, she suspected, the hills would be alive with autumn leaves and burnished sunsets.

Was Texas hers to keep? she wondered. Could she stay here and wait for Bobby to love her the way she loved him? To trust her? To marry her? Or would that be like waiting for a miracle?

A dream that wasn't meant to be.

Thirty minutes later Bobby headed for his office, then stopped in the open doorway.

Julianne sat at his desk, focused on the coffee cup in front of her, as if the liquid inside wielded the power to tell fortunes. She was drinking tea, he assumed. Doctored with cream and sugar.

He watched her, knowing she was unaware of his presence. He liked catching her during quiet, reflective moments, and wondered if she knew how important she'd become to him. How special.

He went to bed every night thinking about her, anticipating the next moment they would spend together. The next smile, the next touch, the next stolen kiss.

Of course, last night had been difficult. After she'd showed up at his place, catching him off guard, he'd struggled to keep the date going, to not feel like a cripple. But he'd gotten through it. He'd survived.

She glanced up and his heart went crazy, striking his chest. A physical reaction he couldn't seem to control, a boyish backlash that made him feel young and stupid.

She didn't smile, but he wasn't smiling, either. He was too busy trying to calm his rebellious heart.

"I've been waiting for you," she said.

He moved forward, reminding himself that he was a man, not a moonstruck kid. "Were you reading tea leaves in the meantime?"

She shifted her cup. "It's milk."

"Oh." The day after they'd made love, he'd bought her favorite tea and stocked the cupboards with it. But milk was a good choice, healthy for the baby. He'd have to remember to replenish the supply. "I hope I didn't keep you waiting long. I had a tour today."

"I know. You guided a group into the hills."

He brushed at his clothes, at the trail dust that lingered. Was this conversation strained? Or was it his imagination? "You seem preoccupied, Julianne."

"I'm afraid, Bobby."

"Of what?" Concerned, he took a chair.

"Of what I need from you. Of things I don't think you're willing to give me."

Nerves tightened, coiling like an unfriendly snake. "Things? You mean, emotional stuff?"

"Yes."

Restless, she twisted her hair, twining it like the anxiety in his gut. He leaned forward, frowned, saw her frown, too.

Was she going to fill him in? Or would she let him sit here and suffer, waiting and wondering?

"Why do you still wear your wedding ring, Bobby?"

The room crashed in on him. He could almost hear books

falling from the shelves, glass shattering from the windows, cutting his skin, making him bleed.

"I just do." Explaining why was impossible. Admitting to Julianne that he and Sharon had argued over the ring just days before she'd died, just days before he'd killed her, wasn't something he could manage.

"You're still in love with her," she said.

No, that wasn't true. He was guilty about his wife. Sickened by what he'd done. "I died the day she died, but I've started living again. I've gone on."

"Have you?" she challenged.

"Yes." How could she ask him something like that? Didn't she see the changes in him? The difference she and the baby had made? "I have a lover again. I have you."

"You won't take your clothes off in front of me. You won't reveal who you are."

With a vile curse, he got to his feet, fighting the urge to punch a wall, the way he used to do when he was a kid. "This is about my leg? About your morbid curiosity to see it?"

Her voice quavered. "There's nothing morbid about my interest in you."

He flexed his fingers, letting the anger go. "You're getting emotional over me, I understand that. I'm getting emotional over you, too. But we're better off leaving things as they are. For God's sake, just let me keep my clothes on."

"Why?"

"Because I need to feel whole around you." He'd treated her badly at his door last night, but her unexpected visit had startled him, embarrassed him, made him feel like a cripple.

And he hated that feeling more than anything.

"You are a whole man, Bobby."

Nice words, he thought. Easy sentiment for someone

who wasn't attaching a prosthetic limb to a stump every morning. "Don't patronize me."

"I'm not. Damn it, I'm not." A defensive light flashed in her eyes, as bright as a diamond, as powerful as flawless stone. "But you never talk about yourself. You never share anything with me."

What was he supposed to confide in her about? The accident? The crushed metal and shattered bones? The blood? The mutilated skin? "If I was in the market for a support group, I'd go to one."

"So that's it? That's all I get? A man who'll sleep with me, but won't open his heart?"

"My heart?" The damned thing was pounding now, beating a painful rhythm. "I thought the issue was my leg. And my ring." He held up his hand, wished he could remove the gold circle from his finger, forget the shame connected to it.

"You don't get it, do you?"

He dropped his hand. "Get what? What is it that I'm not getting, Julianne?"

"That I'm in love with you."

The moment her words hit the air, silence ricocheted.

Fear blasted Bobby like a fist, a set of brass knuckles to the belly. "That wasn't supposed to happen. You weren't supposed to change the rules."

"I didn't do it on purpose." She gripped the handle on her cup. "I swear, I didn't."

Were the rules changing for him, too? Was the need inside him love? The desperation to touch her? To hold her?

God help him, but he wanted to hold her now. Right now, in the midst of the chaos between them.

Bobby looked at her, saw her looking back at him.

"I can't marry you," he said suddenly. He couldn't handle the complication, the ache, the confusion that came with being a husband, with having to protect a wife. "But I would if I could."

Because he loved her. The way she loved him. What point was there in denying it? In pretending that he didn't know the difference between lust and love?

He'd started living again because of her, enjoying simple pleasures, laughing with true mirth, looking forward to waking up each day.

But he still couldn't marry her.

"I love you, too," he said quickly, playing it down, letting her know love wasn't the key to happiness. If anything, it made matters worse, more complicated for both of them. "But the way I feel about you doesn't change anything. I still need my privacy."

"What kind of love is that? Keeping your partner from getting too close?"

"The only kind I have to offer."

Her eyes watered, but she blinked away the obvious emotion. He blinked his away, too.

Stalemate, he thought, remaining true to his convictions, his need to protect himself, to keep his shame and discomfort hidden.

Julianne rose to refill her cup, to give herself a moment to think, a moment to stay strong.

How could she remain in Texas? How could she face each day knowing that she would never be Bobby's wife? That his idea of love conflicted with hers?

On the other hand, how could she leave? Tackle each day without seeing him? Touching him? Holding him?

"I don't know what to do," she blurted, almost spilling her milk.

Bobby remained near the desk, his expression guarded. "What do you mean?"

She turned. "I have to make a decision. Come to terms with all of this."

Panic flashed in his eyes. "You're thinking about going back to Pennsylvania, aren't you?"

"Yes."

"Now? After we both just admitted that we love each other? What kind of logic is that?"

The love he'd offered wasn't enough. Those words meant nothing without compromise, without sacrifice, without commitment. "This is my life we're taking about. My future."

"It's my life, too."

She came forward, placed her cup on the desk. "Yes, but you're expecting me to live by your rules. Rules that don't work for me."

"Damn it." Frustration edged his voice. "A week ago you said you could handle being my lover. I laid my cards on the table and you looked me right in the eye and said you could handle it."

"I know. But that was before I realized I was falling in love with you."

"Love is overrated," he countered, twisting the gold band on his finger. "Women make too damn much of it."

How could he say that? How could he shove her feelings aside? "Before I agreed to move here, I laid *my* cards on the table. I told you that if things didn't work out, I wanted the option to go home."

"And now you're cashing in on that option?"

"I don't know. Maybe." She lifted her milk, took a small sip, willed herself not to cry. He didn't understand how much she needed a commitment from him.

"What about the baby?"

"We'll work something out."

"From across the country?"

"No matter what happens, I won't shut you out of the baby's life. I'm not trying to punish you." But she couldn't punish herself, either. Stay in a situation that pained her.

"God, this hurts." He shoved his left hand into his pocket, as if hiding his ring. "How can you do this? How can you even consider it?"

"Because I love you. And I need for you to love me the same way."

"I do. Damn it. I do."

"No, you don't." And she feared he never would.

He dug his hand deeper into his pocket, burying the ring even farther. "You're judging me. You're assuming what I feel for you isn't real."

Real or not, he didn't covet the same dream as Julianne. He wasn't willing to sacrifice his pride for love, for the kind of intimacy that revealed his soul or unmasked his heart.

"What happens now?" he asked, stepping back, putting yet another distance between them.

"I need some time to think," she told him, already mourning the loss, the closeness they never really had.

Bobby gave her two days and the clock-ticking, hour-lagging time nearly killed him. He couldn't sleep; he couldn't eat; he couldn't work without thinking about her, without hoping and praying she would choose to stay.

At 9:00 p.m. he knocked on her door and Julianne answered right away. She looked tired, pale and vulnerable. But even so, she'd wrapped herself in flowers, in a night-gown with a soft, floral print.

"Hi," he said.

"Hi."

Julianne released an audible breath and he knew she'd

decided to go back to Pennsylvania. To leave him. He could see it on her face, in the shadows beneath her eyes.

He stood tall, guarding his emotions; afraid the pain of losing her would unman him.

She gestured to the living room.

He entered her house and they remained silent.

Finally he lifted his hand. His finger bore a mark in the shape of his ring, where his skin had tanned around it. But regardless, the gold band was gone.

She blinked, did a double take. "You removed it?"

"Yes."

"Why?"

"Because I love you. And it doesn't make any sense to wear a ring another woman gave me."

She took his hand, held it in hers. "Does this mean you'll talk about Sharon now? About the significance of the ring? About why you wore it all those years?"

"No. It just means that I love you."

She released his hand. "You have too many secrets, Bobby. Too many issues you're not willing to share."

Hurt, he squared his shoulders, fought the emptiness in his chest. "This is easy for you, isn't it? Walking away when life get tough."

"Easy?" Her Irish temper flared. "This is the hardest thing I've ever done. But, damn it, I need more from you."

"More than me removing a ring?"

"Yes."

He cursed beneath his breath. Why couldn't it be enough?

"I want to get past Sharon," Julianne said. "I want to see her picture, to hear you say her name without making her seem like a ghost between us."

Sharon wasn't a ghost. She was his cross to bear, his

shame, his remorse. "I wasn't a good husband. My wife deserved better than what she got from me."

Stunned, Julianne stared at him. "Oh, dear God. Did you cheat on her, Bobby? Did you?"

"No."

"Then what?"

He tried to say it, to admit that he'd killed Sharon, but the words wouldn't leave his mouth. "Nothing. Never mind." He faced himself in the mirror every day. He couldn't bear to face Julianne, too. To have her look upon him with disgust.

She shook her head and he knew she was giving up, that she wouldn't push him.

"I booked my flight for next Monday," she said.

A shot of loneliness iced through his veins. "So soon?"

"It hurts too much to stay here." She sank onto the edge of the sofa, as if her legs had gone as weary as her heart.

Bobby wanted to hold her, to pretend this wasn't happening, but he asked about her plans instead. "What about your car?"

"I've arranged to have it transported home, along with the rest of my belongings." She paused, took a breath. "I'm sorry about not following through on the boutique. But I'll give you all of my files. I have a good start."

He didn't care about the store. He wanted his woman. His child.

"And what about our son or daughter?" he asked. "Are we going to shift the baby back and forth?"

"We'll do the best we can. Be the best parents possible."

"I know." But the knowledge that he wouldn't see Julianne and the baby every day was tearing him apart. "Have you worked out everything else? Lined up a job? A new apartment in Pennsylvania?"

"I'm going to stay with Kay and her husband until I rent a place. And I'm not worried about a job. I'll find one."

Of course she would. She was a capable lady. Strong. Independent. Beautiful. "I'll send you a check every month. Enough to—"

"Bobby—"

"Don't argue. Give me this much. Let me help you." *Let me feel as if I matter,* he thought. *As if you can't live without me.*

They looked at each other for a moment and then he said, "I'm going to miss you."

Her eyes watered and her voice broke. "I love you, Bobby. More than you could ever know."

Unable to stop himself, he sat next to her and held out his arms.

But she didn't fall into his embrace. She didn't cry in his arms. Instead she shook her head, refusing the shallow comfort he offered.

Loving each other wasn't enough, he thought.

He looked into her watery eyes and saw her strength, her beauty, the Irish temper that kept her from breaking down.

"I'm sorry," he told her. Sorry he couldn't be the man she needed him to be. That he couldn't marry her.

"You should go," she said, her voice cracking just a little.

Knowing he didn't have a choice, he left the cabin, then stood in the wind and asked the Creator to stop time before Monday.

To keep Julianne here.

Thirteen

————

On Monday, Julianne waited on the porch. Bobby had offered to drive her to the airport and he was due to pick up her up at any moment.

She buttoned her jacket, warding off the moisture in the air. Could she actually go through with this? Could she leave him? Live so far away from the man she loved?

When she saw his truck coming toward the cabin, she hugged herself.

He parked and climbed out of the vehicle. He wore a denim shirt, blue jeans and a brown leather jacket. His hair had been plaited into its usual braid. The brim of a felt cowboy hat shielded his eyes, but he still looked exhausted, as if he'd been battling sleep. She knew how much this was hurting him.

Suddenly she wanted to hold him, to never let go.

''Are you ready?'' he asked.

''Yes.''

He motioned to a leather satchel. "Is this it?"

She nodded. "Everything else is packed in boxes. Maria is going to make sure the moving company has access to them."

Bobby reached for the bag. "Maria doesn't want you to leave."

"I know." The Latina woman had become a dear friend. "I'll come back to visit with the baby. I won't stay away forever."

"I'll keep this house available for you. I won't rent it out again."

She glanced back at the cabin. "You don't have to do that, Bobby."

He started down the porch steps. "I can do whatever I want. I own this place. Besides, I'm going to finish decorating the nursery."

"Yes, of course." But knowing the house would be empty, waiting for her and the baby to return, made her homesick for Texas already. "I feel like I'm leaving a piece of my heart behind."

He stopped, turned to look at her. "Yeah, and you're taking a chunk of mine with you."

Julianne met his troubled gaze. Her decision had broken both of their hearts, leaving them aching for each other.

Then don't go, a voice in her head reasoned. *Stay with him.*

And do what? Remain his desperate lover? The lady he kept at a distance? The lady he refused to marry?

An arrangement like that would only enable Bobby to become more reclusive, to keep more secrets. And eventually it would destroy Julianne's self-worth, her confidence as a woman.

Why couldn't he see that? Why couldn't see how unhealthy it was?

She descended the stairs, clutching her purse strap a little too tightly.

Without speaking, he opened the passenger door for her. She thanked him and buckled her seat belt.

They drove in silence, down country roads, past farms and ranches. She stared out the window and watched the patchwork scenery go by, images of the Texas Hill Country she would never forget.

Finally, when they hit the main highway, the sky opened up, showering the earth with rain.

With tears from heaven, Julianne thought as an unspeakable loneliness crept into her soul.

The windshield wipers swept across the glass and Bobby did his best to remain strong, to tell himself he would survive.

But when he glanced at Julianne, his resolve shattered. She had her hand on her tummy, cradling their baby, the tiny life they'd created.

Tears filled his eyes, but he forced them away, refusing to let her see him cry.

Pride, he thought. His egotistical pride.

He'd killed Sharon with it. And now he was losing Julianne because of it.

He gripped the steering wheel, felt his palms sweat. He couldn't send her away without telling her the truth. Without admitting what he'd done.

He blinked and his gaze fogged. Was it the rain? Or was it his tears?

Suddenly he couldn't see. He couldn't—

Oh, God. What if he killed Julianne and the baby? What if he crashed the truck, rolled it the way he'd done that day?

"I can't do this," he said, releasing the panic. "I can't."

He guided the vehicle to the side of the road, put it in

Park and cut the engine. Then he looked at Julianne, his heart pounding in time to the rain.

"What's going on?" she asked. "What's wrong?"

"If anything ever happened to you, I'd die," he said. "I'd cease to exist."

She gazed at him with confused eyes. "What are you talking about? Nothing is going to happen to me."

"I killed Sharon, Julianne. The accident was my fault." He paused, his stomach clenching. "It was raining that day, too. We were driving back to Texas from Oklahoma, but we were only a few hours from home."

Julianne didn't respond, so he continued, purging his sins.

"When the weather took a turn for the worse, Sharon started to worry. She wanted me to find a motel, so we could wait out the storm."

"But you kept driving."

"Yes. I'd driven in storms much more dangerous than the one we were in. I convinced her everything would be okay. That I'd get her home safe and sound."

He glanced out the windshield, recalling how macho he'd been, how sure of himself. "About thirty minutes later a vehicle behind us lost control and in the chaos that followed, several cars swerved. Someone sideswiped us and I skidded across the wet highway and went off an embankment."

Bobby closed his eyes. Julianne remained quiet, listening to him describe the day he'd killed his wife. "Our truck rolled, pinning us inside." He could still feel the slow-motion effect of the crash, the mangled metal, the break of his own bones, the trauma of his leg being partially severed. "I didn't see what happened to Sharon. I passed out and when I regained consciousness, I was in the hospital." He sucked in a breath, forced it out of his lungs. "She didn't stand a chance. She died at the scene of the accident."

He opened his eyes, stared straight ahead. "We'd been visiting her family in Oklahoma. And I'd just promised her parents that I would take care of their daughter, that I would protect her."

"It was an accident. You didn't mean for her to die."

He turned toward Julianne, confused by her expression, by the tenderness and compassion. She wasn't looking at him at if he were some sort of monster. She didn't see the ugliness inside him.

"I still love you," she said, as if reading his mind. "This doesn't change how I feel about you."

"How can you say that?"

"Because you're a good man with a good heart. And now I understand what you've been going through. The guilt and pain you've had to bear."

Bobby squeezed her hand, held it like a lifeline. He wondered what he'd done to deserve her, to have such a beautiful woman believe in him.

Nothing, he thought, guilt consuming him again. He didn't deserve Julianne's support.

"I wasn't wearing my wedding band on the day Sharon died," he admitted, explaining why the ring had become an issue. "About a week before our trip to Oklahoma, I injured my hand. It wasn't a serious injury, but I removed my ring because my fingers started to swell. After my hand healed, I—"

"Didn't want to put your ring back on," Julianne provided gently.

Bobby nodded, shame curling in his belly. "I was restoring a vintage truck at the time and my ring was getting in the way. I was concerned about another injury."

He blew a breath. "Sharon got upset. Really upset. I

couldn't understand her logic, why she was making such a fuss. I told her that a lot of men didn't wear their wedding bands. Construction workers, mechanics, guys who did physical labor.'' He paused, glanced at his empty finger. ''After she died, I put the ring back on. I had Michael bring it to me in the hospital.'' Out of guilt, he thought. Out of remorse. ''That gold band was a reminder of what I'd done. Of the day I'd taken her life.''

''Oh, Bobby.'' Julianne raised their joined hands and brushed his knuckles with her lips. ''You never let yourself feel anything but pain. Nothing good. No positive memories.''

''She was so young. She'd just graduated from college. How was I supposed to face what I'd done?''

''You didn't do anything but love her.''

The guilt returned, constricting his chest. ''I should have listened to her. I should have found a motel, waited out the storm.''

''You made a mistake. And you paid dearly for that mistake.''

''I deserved to pay.''

''No, you didn't,'' she argued softly. ''You had the right to mourn your wife, but you also had the right to find peace. To go on.''

Did he? Bobby wondered. Was it that simple?

He looked at Julianne. He wanted to be with her, to raise their child together, to share joys and sorrows, to celebrate holidays, to dance, to laugh, to cuddle on long winter nights.

''I'm willing to start living now,'' he said, knowing he couldn't bear to lose her. ''To stop holding back. To give you my heart.''

Reacting to his words, to his need for her, Julianne

leaned toward him and he stroked her hair. His lady. His love. The Irish fairy who touched his soul.

"Will you stay in Texas?" he asked. "Will you come back to the ranch with me?"

She lifted her head, her lashes glistening with tears.

Their gazes locked and he waited for her answer. He knew this was what he wanted, what he needed.

But he couldn't propose, not yet. That would come later, when the timing was right. When he faced the next hurdle.

"Will you?" he repeated his question, asking her to return to the ranch with him.

Her voice broke. "I'd be honored to."

Bobby's heart stuck in his throat.

He glanced at the windshield. The rain had lessened, but the roads were still wet. "Do you trust me to get you home safely?"

"Yes," she told him, looking directly into his eyes. "I trust you with my life."

Julianne and Bobby arrived at her cabin. He'd stopped by his place to pack a bag and to grab his crutches, which meant he was willing to stay the night.

But even so, Julianne sensed he was apprehensive about his leg, still concerned about revealing it to her.

They entered her house in silence and she wished this wasn't so awkward, that she knew what to say or to do to make this moment more natural.

Should she turn to him? Kiss him? Lead him to her room? Or would that be too aggressive?

She closed the door and he moved closer. Without thinking, without worrying any more, she slipped her arms around his neck.

Their mouths came together, softly, gently.

As warm as her heart. As moist as the rain.

"I don't want to wait until tonight," she said. She wanted him now. All of him. Every solid muscle, every bone-sturdy ridge, every virile plane.

"Me, either." He deepened the kiss, then stepped back. "I'll use the other bathroom. It'll be easier that way."

He wanted privacy, she realized. Time to psyche himself into removing his prosthesis.

She took a breath, summoned a smile. "Are you going to meet me in the bedroom?"

"Yes. I'll be ready in just a bit." He returned her smile, but she knew he was still nervous.

Julianne was nervous, too. She wanted this to be special.

After he retreated down the hall, she headed to the master bathroom. She slipped on the prettiest nightgown she owned and lit some scented candles, hoping Bobby would appreciate the romantic ambience.

Waiting on the edge of the bed like a virgin bride, she twisted her hands on her lap. Maybe she was trying too hard. Maybe she should have worn a pair of panties. Maybe—

Bobby came into the room on his crutches and her heart went soft and girlish.

He wore a pair of boxers and nothing else. His hair, loose and combed away from his face, fell across his shoulders and down his back.

She longed to touch him, to hold him, feel his bare skin against hers. She glanced at his amputated leg, accepting the strength and beauty of it.

Bobby Elk spent his days running a guest ranch, training riders, enjoying the horses that kept him focused, battling his disability like a true American cowboy.

"You're perfect," she said.

"Perfect?" He tilted his head. "You must need glasses, dear lady."

"Are you accusing me of getting old, Mr. Elk? Of not being able to recognize a hunky guy when I see one?"

He laughed and moved forward, then stopped and made a troubled face. "I wish I could carry you to bed, Julianne. I wish I wasn't standing here with these damn crutches under my arms."

"That doesn't matter. Just lie down with me. Hold me."

They climbed into bed and he held her against his chest. For the longest time they remained quiet. He stroked her hair and she closed her eyes.

"I didn't ask you earlier," he said. "But I wanted to wait until we were in bed. Until you knew what you were in for."

She opened her eyes. "Ask me what?"

"To marry me."

Julianne touched his face, tracing the features she'd come to know, the features she hoped their child would inherit. "Are you asking me now?"

"Yes."

Tears misted. Happy tears. Emotional tears. "I've been waiting for this. Hoping and praying."

He smiled and she brushed his lips with a tender kiss. He was everything her heart wanted, everything her soul ached to claim.

Anxious, she deepened the kiss, feeding on his mouth, his tongue, the thrill of knowing he belonged to her.

Bobby hadn't expected the flash of heat. He'd pictured shy advances, with Julianne avoiding his residual limb, trying to be polite.

But her hands were everywhere, sliding all over his body. He didn't have time to feel self-conscious, to give a damn that part of his leg was missing.

She rubbed against him and he grinned and streaked a

hand under her nightgown, suddenly aware that she was naked underneath.

He stroked her, making her wet and slick. She arched and moaned, inviting him to absorb her breathy pants, her dreamy sighs, her sweet, sweet need.

When she climaxed, he watched her, fascinated by the tremor in her body, the emerald glow in her eyes.

She reached for his boxers and he helped her remove them. While she straddled him, she lifted her nightgown over her head and let it float to the floor.

She looked like a goddess, pale skin glowing by candlelight, vibrant hair tangling like scarlet vines.

He circled the tips of her breasts and she leaned forward to kiss him, to taste his tongue.

And then she lifted her hips and impaled herself on his length, intensifying every sensation, every thundering beat of his heart.

Time and space disappeared. There was nothing but the rhythm of sexual surrender pumping through his blood, the rise of scented smoke swirling in the air.

He slid his hands along her curves, encouraging her to ride him slow and easy, then strong and steady, then hard and fast.

He wanted it all. Every hot, searing kiss, every quick, driving motion, every spiraling lash of pleasure.

Their eyes locked and he reared up to claim her, to brand her, to thrust deep.

She clawed his shoulders; he licked the side of her neck, more aroused than he'd ever been.

She arched and bucked, and he spilled into her, joining her in a hot, hammering orgasm.

Afterward she collapsed on top of him and for the longest time, neither of them moved.

Finally he slipped his arm around her, cradling her, keeping her warm and protected.

She sighed and he marveled at the silkiness of her skin, the tickle of her hair against his chin. Being this close to Julianne was the most incredible feeling in the world.

A feeling of strength, of wholeness, where nothing was missing, neither from his heart nor his body.

She shifted, pressing her cheek against his chest, and he stroked her back, sliding his hand up and down her spine

A-tsi-ye-hi, he thought. Soon she would take a vow with him, become his wife.

"It's going to be okay," she said.

He nuzzled the top of her head. "Yes, it is." Because of her. Because she would help him heal, help him find a way to cope with the past.

It would get easier, Bobby thought. Every day would bring new meaning, new emotions, new challenges.

"I'm looking forward to the future," he said.

"So am I." She took his hand and placed it on her tummy, reminding him of the baby in her womb. "I love you, Bobby."

"I love you, too." He watched the candles flicker, then shifted to kiss her.

To join with her again.

And again, he thought. For the rest of their lives.

Epilogue

Julianne reclined in a hospital bed, weary and sore, but too excited to sleep, to lose sight of the wonder surrounding her.

After a long and exhausting labor, she'd given birth to an eight-pound baby boy. And now the child lay in her arms, wrapped in a blanket. She and Bobby had known ahead of time that their child was a boy, but that hadn't prepared them for the sheer and total awe of this moment.

Bobby stood beside the bed, with pride and emotion in his eyes.

Her lover. Her husband.

On a breezy fall morning they'd been married in an idyllic ceremony in the hills, exchanging vows beneath the vast Texas sky, with friends and family in attendance. She'd carried a single white rose and he'd give her a blue diamond, a ring as bright and magical as an enchanted star.

It had been the most joyous event of her life.

Just like today.

He reached for a colorful bag. "I found this in the gift shop."

"Another teddy bear?" she asked. He'd started a collection for their baby months ago, adding furry little faces to the nursery nearly every week.

"I couldn't resist." He lifted the toy. "This one comes with a song." He wound the key on the side and filled the room with a lullaby.

"It's beautiful." And so was he, this man who said Cherokee prayers every morning.

While the music played, he sat on the edge of the bed, lowered his head and initiated a kiss.

He tasted of quiet days and romantic nights, of the ranch he'd built, of the dreams they shared.

They'd put the past behind them, the ghost that used to haunt them. Bobby spoke of Sharon easily now, convinced that she would be glad he'd moved on, that guilt no longer wracked his soul.

Julianne had made peace with Sharon, too. She'd seen the other woman's picture, her dark eyes, her long dark hair. They were nothing alike, but they'd loved the same man. And somehow, that was enough.

He moved back to touch their son's cheek, to trace each tiny feature. "He's amazing. Incredible. Everything I'd imagined he would be."

"For me, too." The baby she'd always longed for.

Bobby moved closer. "He looks like a magical little bird. A raven. I don't suppose we could name him that, though."

She smoothed a hand over the boy's thick black hair. She'd known that Bobby didn't want to choose a name until the child was born, until they saw him.

"What do you think?" he asked.

"It's your choice," she told him. His duty as a Cherokee father.

"I want you to be part of this. I want him to have a name that reflects you, too."

Touched, she looked at Bobby, knowing how significant this was to him. "An Irish name for a Cherokee baby." A mixed-blood with his daddy's golden skin and deep-set eyes. "How about Brendan? It means little raven."

"Really?" He reached for the baby and rocked the sleeping infant against his chest. "Brendan Elk. That's perfect."

"Brendan *Robert* Elk," she added, honoring her husband.

He looked up and smiled, and she put her hand on his knee, encouraging him to cuddle next to her.

And in the silence that followed they admired their newborn son, their little raven—the child who'd brought them together, who made their lives sparkle with love and beauty. With the promise, she thought, of happily ever after.

* * * * *

*Look for Michael Elk's story
coming in July from Silhouette Desire.*

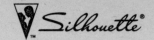

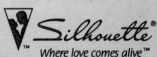

If you enjoyed what you just read,
then we've got an offer you can't resist!

Take 2 bestselling
love stories FREE!

Plus get a FREE surprise gift!

Clip this page and mail it to Silhouette Reader Service™

IN U.S.A.
3010 Walden Ave.
P.O. Box 1867
Buffalo, N.Y. 14240-1867

IN CANADA
P.O. Box 609
Fort Erie, Ontario
L2A 5X3

YES! Please send me 2 free Silhouette Desire® novels and my free surprise gift. After receiving them, if I don't wish to receive anymore, I can return the shipping statement marked cancel. If I don't cancel, I will receive 6 brand-new novels every month, before they're available in stores! In the U.S.A., bill me at the bargain price of $3.57 plus 25¢ shipping and handling per book and applicable sales tax, if any*. In Canada, bill me at the bargain price of $4.24 plus 25¢ shipping and handling per book and applicable taxes**. That's the complete price and a savings of at least 10% off the cover prices—what a great deal! I understand that accepting the 2 free books and gift places me under no obligation ever to buy any books. I can always return a shipment and cancel at any time. Even if I never buy another book from Silhouette, the 2 free books and gift are mine to keep forever.

225 SDN DNUP
326 SDN DNUQ

Name	(PLEASE PRINT)	
Address	Apt.#	
City	State/Prov.	Zip/Postal Code

* Terms and prices subject to change without notice. Sales tax applicable in N.Y.
** Canadian residents will be charged applicable provincial taxes and GST.
   All orders subject to approval. Offer limited to one per household and not valid to current Silhouette Desire® subscribers.
   ® are registered trademarks of Harlequin Books S.A., used under license.

DES02   ©1998 Harlequin Enterprises Limited

COMING NEXT MONTH

#1513 SHAMELESS—Ann Major
Lone Star Country Club
With danger nipping at her heels, Celeste Cavanaugh turned to rancher Phillip Westin, her very capable, very *good-looking* ex. Though Phillip still drove her crazy with his take-charge ways, it wasn't long before he and Celeste were back in each other's arms. But this time Celeste was playing for keeps…and she was shamelessly in love!

#1514 BEAUTY & THE BLUE ANGEL—Maureen Child
Dynasties: The Barones
When soon-to-be-single-mom Daisy Cusack went into labor on the job, help came in the form of sexy navy pilot Alex Barone. Before she knew it, Daisy was in danger of falling for her handsome white knight. Alex was everything she'd dreamed of, but what would happen when his leave ended?

#1515 PRINCESS IN HIS BED—Leanne Banks
The Royal Dumonts
The minute he saw the raven-haired beauty who'd crashed into his barn, rancher Jared McNeil knew he was in trouble. Then Mimi Deerman agreed to work off her debt by caring for his nieces. Jared sensed Mimi had secrets, but playing house with her had undeniable benefits, and Jared soon longed to make their temporary arrangement permanent. Little did he know that his elegant nanny was really a princess in disguise!

#1516 THE GENTRYS: ABBY—Linda Conrad
The Gentrys
Though Comanche Gray Wolf Parker had vowed not to get involved with a woman not chosen by his tribal elders, after green-eyed Abby Gentry saved his life, he was honor-bound to help her. When Abby's brother tried to arrange a marriage for her, Gray suggested a pretend engagement. But the heat they generated was all too real, and Gray was torn between love and duty.

#1517 MAROONED WITH A MILLIONAIRE—Kristi Gold
The Baby Bank
The last thing millionaire recluse Jackson Dunlap wanted was the company of spunky, pregnant Lizzie Matheson. But after he rescued the fun-loving blond enchantress from a hot-air balloon and they wound up stranded on his boat, he found himself utterly defenseless against her many charms. If he didn't know better, he'd say he was falling in love!

#1518 SLEEPING WITH THE PLAYBOY—Julianne MacLean
Sleeping with her client was *not* part of bodyguard Jocelyn MacKenzie's job description, but Donovan Knight was pure temptation. The charismatic millionaire made her feel feminine *and* powerful, but if they were to have a future together, Jocelyn would have to confront her fears and insecurities…and finally lay them to rest.

SDCNM0503